PRAISE FOR *BRIGHT LIGHTS, BIG CITY*

"Funny and fast-paced . . . It's perfect for anyone who has ever found himself on the street at 6 in the morning after dancing all night with the wrong person."
—*THE NEW YORK TIMES*

"Terrific: remarkable, funny writing, a perfect power-to-weight ratio."
—THOMAS McGUANE

"A very funny, oddly touching book, and something of a tour de force as well . . . McInerney not only jests at our slightly tawdry life, but also celebrates its abiding possibilities."
—*NEW REPUBLIC*

"Remarkable . . . McInerney has an incredible ability to pack more substance into one sentence than most writers are able to convey in ten."
—*MADEMOISELLE*

"Engagingly modest, funny, perfectly balanced."
—*THE NEW YORK REVIEW OF BOOKS*

"*Bright Lights* is the book to read."
—*USA TODAY*

"Very funny and shrewd . . . Great windsprint passages that leave tattered mystiques in their wake."
—*VILLAGE VOICE*

BOOKS BY JAY McINERNEY
Ransom
Bright Lights, Big City

BRIGHT
LIGHTS,
BIG
CITY

BRIGHT LIGHTS, BIG CITY

A NOVEL BY

JAY McINERNEY

VINTAGE BOOKS

A DIVISION OF RANDOM HOUSE

NEW YORK

Vintage Books Edition, December 1987

Library of Congress Cataloging-in-Publication Data
McInerney, Jay.
  Bright lights, big city.
  I. Title.
PS3563.C3694B7   1987   813'.54   87-40270
ISBN 0-394-75688-6 (pbk.)

Portions of this work were previously published in the *Paris
Review* and *Ploughshares*. Grateful acknowledgment is made
to Index Music, Inc., for permission to reprint an excerpt
from the lyrics to "Cross-Eyed and Painless" by David Byrne
and Brian Eno. Copyright © 1980 Bleu Disque Music Co.,
Inc., Index Music, Inc., and E.G. Music, Ltd., by permission of David Byrne and Brian Eno.

All of the events and characters
depicted in this book are fictional.

Book design by Jessica Shatan

Manufactured in the United States of America
10 9 8 7 6 5 4 3 2

FOR
MY
MOTHER
AND
FATHER,
AND
FOR
MERRY

"How did you go bankrupt?" Bill asked.
"Two ways," Mike said. "Gradually and then suddenly."
—THE SUN ALSO RISES

CONTENTS

BRIGHT LIGHTS, BIG CITY

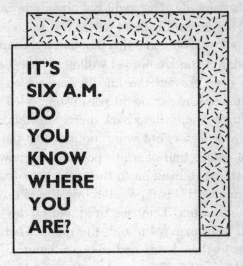

**IT'S
SIX A.M.
DO
YOU
KNOW
WHERE
YOU
ARE?**

You are not the kind of guy who would be at a place like this at this time of the morning. But here you are, and you cannot say that the terrain is entirely unfamiliar, although the details are fuzzy. You are at a nightclub talking to a girl with a shaved head. The club is either Heartbreak or the Lizard Lounge. All might come clear if you could just slip into the bathroom and do a little more Bolivian Marching Powder. Then again, it might not. A small voice inside you insists that this epidemic lack of clarity is a result of too much

3

of that already. The night has already turned on that imperceptible pivot where two A.M. changes to six A.M. You know this moment has come and gone, but you are not yet willing to concede that you have crossed the line beyond which all is gratuitous damage and the palsy of unraveled nerve endings. Somewhere back there you could have cut your losses, but you rode past that moment on a comet trail of white powder and now you are trying to hang on to the rush. Your brain at this moment is composed of brigades of tiny Bolivian soldiers. They are tired and muddy from their long march through the night. There are holes in their boots and they are hungry. They need to be fed. They need the Bolivian Marching Powder.

A vaguely tribal flavor to this scene—pendulous jewelry, face paint, ceremonial headgear and hair styles. You feel that there is also a certain Latin theme—something more than the piranhas cruising your bloodstream and the fading buzz of marimbas in your brain.

You are leaning back against a post that may or may not be structural with regard to the building, but which feels essential to your own maintenance of an upright position. The bald girl is saying this used to be a good place to come before the assholes discovered it. You don't want to be talking to this bald girl, or even listening to her, which is all you are doing, but just now you do not want to test the powers of speech or loco-motion.

How did you get here? It was your friend, Tad Allagash, who powered you in here, and he has disappeared. Tad is the kind of guy who would be at a place like this at this time of the morning. He is either your best self or your worst self, you're not sure which. Earlier in the evening it seemed clear that he was your best self. You started on the Upper East Side with champagne and unlimited prospects, strictly observing the Allagash rule of perpetual motion: one drink per stop. Tad's mission in life is to have more fun than anyone else in New York City, and this in-volves a lot of moving around, since there is al-ways the likelihood that where you aren't is more fun than where you are. You are awed by his strict refusal to acknowledge any goal higher than the pursuit of pleasure. You want to be like that. You also think he is shallow and dangerous. His friends are all rich and spoiled, like the cousin from Memphis you met earlier in the evening who would not accompany you below Fourteenth Street because, he said, he didn't have a lowlife visa. This cousin had a girlfriend with cheekbones to break your heart, and you knew she was the

real thing when she steadfastly refused to acknowledge your presence. She possessed secrets—about islands, about horses, about French
pronunciation—that you would never know.

You have traveled in the course of the night
from the meticulous to the slime. The girl with
the shaved head has a scar tattooed on her scalp.
It looks like a long, sutured gash. You tell her it
is very realistic. She takes this as a compliment
and thanks you. You meant as opposed to romantic.

"I could use one of those right over my heart,"
you say.

"You want I can give you the name of the guy
that did it. You'd be surprised how cheap."

You don't tell her that nothing would surprise
you now. Her voice, for instance, which is like
the New Jersey State Anthem played through an
electric shaver.

The bald girl is emblematic of the problem.
The problem is, for some reason you think you
are going to meet the kind of girl who is not the
kind of girl who would be at a place like this at
this time of the morning. When you meet her
you are going to tell her that what you really
want is a house in the country with a garden.
New York, the club scene, bald women—you're
tired of all that. Your presence here is only a

matter of conducting an experiment in limits, reminding yourself of what you aren't. You see yourself as the kind of guy who wakes up early on Sunday morning and steps out to cop the *Times* and croissants. Who might take a cue from the Arts and Leisure section and decide to check out an exhibition—costumes of the Hapsburg Court at the Met, say, or Japanese lacquerware of the Muromachi period at the Asia Society. The kind of guy who calls up the woman he met at a publishing party Friday night, the party he did not get sloppy drunk at. See if she wants to check out the exhibition and maybe do an early dinner. A guy who would wait until eleven A.M. to call her, because she might not be an early riser, like he is. She may have been out late, perhaps at a nightclub. And maybe a couple of sets of tennis before the museum. He wonders if she plays, but of course she would.

When you meet the girl who wouldn't et cetera you will tell her that you are slumming, visiting your own six A.M. Lower East Side of the soul on a lark, stepping nimbly between the piles of garbage to the gay marimba rhythms in your head. Well, no, not *gay*. But she will know exactly what you mean.

On the other hand, almost any girl, specifically one with a full head of hair, would help you stave off this creeping sense of mortality. You remember the Bolivian Marching Powder and realize you're not down yet. No way, José. First you have to get rid of this bald girl.

◩

In the bathroom there are no doors on the stalls, which makes it tough to be discreet. But clearly you are not the only person in here to take on fuel. Lots of sniffling going on in the stalls. The windows are blacked over, and for this you are profoundly grateful.

Hup, two, three, four. The soldiers are back on their feet. They are off and running in formation. Some of them are dancing, and you must follow their example.

Just outside the door you spot her: tall, dark and alone, half hidden behind a pillar at the edge of the dance floor. You approach laterally, moving your stuff like a Bad Spade through the slalom of a synthesized conga rhythm. She jumps when you touch her shoulder.

"Dance?"

She looks at you as if you had just suggested instrumental rape. "I do not speak English," she says, when you ask again.

"Français?"

She shakes her head. Why is she looking at you that way, as if tarantulas were nesting in your eye sockets?

"You are by any chance from Bolivia? Or Peru?"

She is looking around for help now. Remembering a recent encounter with a young heiress's bodyguard at Danceteria—or was it the Red Parrot?—you back off, hands raised over your head.

The Bolivian Soldiers are still on their feet, but they have stopped singing their marching song. You realize that you are at a crucial juncture vis-à-vis morale. What you need is a good pep talk from Tad Allagash, but he is not to be found. You try to imagine what he would say. *Back on the horse. Now we're really going to have some fun.* Something like that. You suddenly realize that he has already slipped out with some rich Hose Queen. He is back at her place on Fifth Avenue, and they are doing some of her off-the-boat-quality drugs. They are scooping it out of tall Ming vases and snorting it off of each other's naked bodies. You hate Tad Allagash.

Go home. Cut your losses.

Stay. Go for it.

You are a republic of voices tonight. Unfortunately, that republic is Italy. All these voices waving their arms and screaming at one another. There's an *ex cathedra* riff coming down from the

9

Vatican: *Repent. Your body is the temple of the Lord and you have defiled it*. It is, after all, Sunday morning, and as long as you have any brain cells left there will be a resonant patriarchal basso echoing down the marble vaults of your churchgoing childhood to remind you that this is the Lord's Day. What you need is another overpriced drink to drown it out. But a search of pockets yields only a dollar bill and change. You paid twenty to get in here. Panic gains.

You spot a girl at the edge of the dance floor who looks like your last chance for earthly salvation. You know for a fact that if you go out into the morning alone, without even your sunglasses—which you have neglected to bring, because who, after all, plans on these travesties?—the harsh, angling light will turn you to flesh and bone. Mortality will pierce you through the retina. But there she is in her pegged pants, a kind of doo-wop Retro ponytail pulled off to the side, as eligible a candidate as you are likely to find this late in the game. The sexual equivalent of fast food.

She shrugs and nods when you ask her to dance. You like the way she moves, the oiled ellipses of her hips and shoulders. After the second song, she says she's tired. She's at the point of bolting when you ask her if she needs a little pick-me-up.

"You've got some blow?" she says.

"Is Stevie Wonder blind?" you say.

She takes your arm and leads you into the Ladies'. A couple of spoons and she seems to like you just fine, and you are feeling very likable yourself. A couple more. This woman is all nose.

"I love drugs," she says, as you march toward the bar.

"It's something we have in common," you say.

"Have you ever noticed how all the good words start with D? D and L."

You try to think about this. You're not quite sure what she's driving at. The Bolivians are singing their marching song, but you can't make out the words.

"You know. Drugs. Delight. Decadence."

"Debauchery," you say, catching the tune now.

"Dexedrine."

"Delectable. Deranged. Debilitated."

"Delinquent."

"Delirium."

"And L," she says. "Lush and luscious."

"Languorous."

"Librium."

"Libidinous."

"What's that?" she says.

"Horny."

"Oh," she says, casting a long, arching look over your shoulder. Her eyes glaze in a way that reminds you precisely of the closing of a sand-blasted glass shower door. You can see that the game is over, although you're not sure which rule you broke. Possibly she finds H words offensive. A purist. She is scanning the dance floor for a man with a compatible vocabulary. You have more: *detumescence,* for instance. *Drowning* and *de-pressed; lost* and *lonesome.* It's not that you're really going to miss this girl who thinks that *decadence* and *Dexedrine* are the high points of the language of Kings James and Lear. But the touch of flesh, the sound of another human voice . . . You know there is a special purgatory waiting for you out there in the dawn's surly light, a desperate half sleep which is like a grease fire in the brainpan.

The girl waves as she disappears into the crowd. There is no sign of the other girl, the girl who would not be here. There is no sign of Tad Allagash. The Bolivians are mutinous. You can't stop their treacherous voices.

It is worse even than you expected, stepping out into the morning. The glare is like a mother's reproach. The sidewalk sparkles cruelly. Visibility unlimited. The downtown warehouses look serene and restful in this beveled light. An uptown cab passes and you start to wave, then realize you have no money. The cab stops.

You jog over and lean in the window. "I guess I'll walk after all."

"Asshole." He leaves rubber.

You start north, holding a hand over your eyes. Trucks rumble up Hudson Street, bearing provisions into the sleeping city. You turn east. On Seventh Avenue an old woman with a hive of rollers on her head walks a German shepherd. The dog is rooting in the cracks of the sidewalk, but as you approach he stiffens into a pose of terrible alertness. The woman looks at you as if you were something that had just crawled out of the ocean trailing ooze and slime. An eager, tentative growl ripples the shepherd's throat. "Good Pooky," she says. The dog makes a move but she chokes it back. You give them a wide berth.

On Bleecker Street you catch the scent of the Italian bakery. You stand at the corner of Bleecker and Cornelia and gaze at the windows on the fourth floor of a tenement. Behind those windows is the apartment you shared with Amanda when you first came to New York. It was small and dark, but you liked the imperfectly patched pressed-tin ceiling, the claw-footed bath in the kitchen, the windows that didn't quite fit the frames. You were just starting out. You had the rent covered, you had your favorite restaurant on MacDougal where the waitresses knew your names and you could bring your own bottle of wine. Every morning you woke to the smell of bread from the bakery downstairs. You would go out to buy the paper and maybe pick up a couple of croissants while Amanda made the coffee. This was two years ago, before you got married.

Down on the West Side Highway, a lone hooker totters on heels and tugs at her skirt as if no one had told her that the commuters won't be coming through the tunnels from Jersey today. Coming closer, you see that she is a man in drag.

You cross under the rusting stanchions of the old elevated highway and walk out to the pier. The easterly light skims across the broad expanse of the Hudson. You step carefully as you approach the end of the rotting pier. You are none too steady and there are holes through which you can see the black, fetid water underneath.

You sit down on a piling and look out over the river. Downriver, the Statue of Liberty shimmers in the haze. Across the water, a huge Colgate sign welcomes you to New Jersey, the Garden State.

You watch the solemn progress of a garbage barge, wreathed in a cloud of screaming gulls, heading out to sea.

Here you are again. All messed up and no place to go.

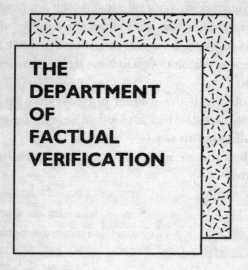

THE
DEPARTMENT
OF
FACTUAL
VERIFICATION

Monday arrives on schedule. You sleep through the first ten hours. God only knows what happened to Sunday.

At the subway station you wait fifteen minutes on the platform for a train. Finally a local, enervated by graffiti, shuffles into the station. You get a seat and hoist a copy of the *New York Post*. The *Post* is the most shameful of your several addictions. You hate to support this kind of trash with your thirty cents, but you are a secret fan of Killer Bees, Hero Cops, Sex Fiends, Lottery

Winners, Teenage Terrorists, Liz Taylor, Tough Tots, Sicko Creeps, Living Nightmares, Life on Other Planets, Spontaneous Human Combustion, Miracle Diets and Coma Babies. The Coma Baby is on page two: COMA BABY SIS PLEADS: SAVE MY LITTLE BROTHER. There is a picture of a four- or five-year-old girl with a dazed expression. She is the living daughter of a pregnant woman who, after an automobile accident, has been lying in a coma for a week. The question that has confronted *Post* readers for days is whether or not the Coma Baby will ever see the light of the delivery room.

The train shudders and pitches toward Fourteenth Street, stopping twice for breathers in the tunnel. You are reading about Liz Taylor's new boyfriend when a sooty hand taps your shoulder. You do not have to look up to know you are facing a casualty, one of the city's MIAs. You are more than willing to lay some silver on the physically handicapped, but folks with the long-distance eyes give you the heebie-jeebies.

The second time he taps your shoulder you look up. His clothes and hair are fairly neat, as if he had only recently let go of social convention, but his eyes are out-to-lunch and his mouth is working furiously.

"My birthday," he says, "is January thirteenth.

I will be twenty-nine years old." Somehow he makes this sound like a threat to kill you with a blunt object.

"Great," you say, going back to the paper.

When you next look up the man is halfway down the car, staring intently at an ad for a business training institute. As you watch, he sits down in the lap of an old lady. She tries to get out from under him but he has her pinned.

"Excuse me, sir, but you're sitting on me," she says. "Sir, sir. Excuse me." Almost everyone in the car is watching and pretending they're not. The man folds his arms across his chest and leans farther back.

"Sir, please get off of me."

You can't even believe it. Half a dozen healthy men are within spitting distance. You would have jumped up yourself but you assumed someone closer to the action would act. The woman is quietly sobbing. As each moment passes it becomes harder and harder to do anything without calling attention to the fact that you hadn't done anything earlier. You keep hoping the man will stand up and leave her alone. You imagine the headline in the *Post:* GRANNY CRUSHED BY NUT WHILE WIMPS WATCH.

"Please, sir."

You stand up. At the same time, the man stands up. He brushes his coat with his hands and then walks down to the far end of the car. You feel silly standing there. The old lady is dabbing at her eyes with a Kleenex. You would like to see if she's all right, but at this point it wouldn't do much good. You sit down.

It's ten-fifty when you get to Times Square. You come up on Seventh Avenue blinking. The sunlight is excessive. You grope for your shades. Down Forty-second Street, through the meat district. Every day the same spiel from the same old man: "Girls, girls, girls—check 'em out, check 'em out. Take a free look, gentlemen. Check it out, check it out." The words and rhythm never vary. Kinky Karla, Naughty Lola, Sexsational Live Revue—girls, girls, girls.

Waiting for a light at Forty-second, you scope among the announcements of ancient upcoming events, strangling the lamppost like kudzu, a fresh poster with the headline MISSING PERSON. The photograph shows a smiling, toothy girl, circa Junior Prom. You read: *Mary O'Brien McCann; NYU student; blue eyes, brown hair, last seen vicinity Washington Square Park, wearing blue jumper, white blouse.* Your heart sinks. You think of those left behind, the dazed loved ones who have hand-lettered this sign and taped it here, who will probably never know what happened. The light has changed.

You stop at the corner for a doughnut and coffee to go. It's 10:58. You've worn out the line about the subway breaking down. Maybe tell Clara you stopped to take a free look at Kinky Karla and got bitten by her snake.

Into the lobby, your chest constricting in anticipation, your throat getting dry. You used to feel this way walking into school Monday mornings. The dread of not having finished your homework—and where were you going to sit at lunch? It didn't help being the new kid every year. The stale disinfectant smell of the corridors and the hard faces of teachers. Your boss, Clara Tillinghast, somewhat resembles a fourth-grade tyrant, one of those ageless disciplinarians who believe that little boys are evil and little girls frivolous, that an idle mind is the devil's playground and that learning is the pounding of facts, like so many nails, into the knotty oak of recalcitrant heads. Ms. Clara Tillinghast, aka Clingfast, aka The Clinger, runs the Department of Factual Verification like a spelling class, and lately you have not accumulated many gold stars. You are hanging on by the skin of your chipped teeth. If the Clinger had her way you would have been expelled long ago, but the magazine has a tradition of never acknowledging its mistakes. The folk history of the place has it that no one has ever been fired: not the narcoleptic theater critic who confused two different off-Broadway premieres and ran a review that combined elements of a Southern family saga and a farce about Vietnam; not the award-winning plagiarist who cribbed a five-thousand-word piece direct from a twenty-year-old issue of *Punch* and signed her name to it. It's a lot like the Ivy League, from which its staff is mostly drawn, or like a cold, impenetrable New England family which keeps even the black sheep suffocating within the fold. You, however, are a minor cousin at best; if there were a branch of the family business in a distant, malarial colony, you would have been shipped off long ago, *sans* quinine. Your transgressions are numerous. You can't call them specifically to mind, but Clingfast has the list in one of her file cabinets. She takes it out from time to time and reads you excerpts. Clara has a mind like a steel mousetrap and a heart like a twelve-minute egg.

Lucio, the elevator operator, says good morning. He was born in Sicily and has been doing this for seventeen years. With a week's training he could probably take over your job and then you could ride the elevator up and down all day long. You're at the twenty-ninth floor in no time. Say so long to Lucio, hello to Sally, the receptionist, perhaps the only staffer with a low-rent accent. She's from one of the outer boroughs, comes in via bridge or tunnel. Generally people here speak as if they were weaned on Twinings English Breakfast Tea. Tillinghast picked up her broad vowels and karate-chop consonants at Vassar. She's very sensitive about coming from Nevada. The writers, of course, are another story—foreigners and other unclubbables among them—but they come and go from their thirtieth-floor cubbyholes at strange hours. They pass manuscripts under the doors at night, and duck into empty offices if they spot you coming at them down the hallway. One mystery man up there—the Ghost—has been working on an article for seven years.

The editorial offices cover two floors. Sales and advertising are several floors below, the division emphasizing the strict independence of art and commerce in the institution. They wear suits on twenty-five, speak a different language and have carpeting on the floors, lithographs on the walls. You are not supposed to talk to them. Up here, the air is too rarefied to support broadloom, the style a down-at-the-heels hauteur. A shoeshine or an overly insistent trouser press is suspect, quite possibly Italian. The layout suggests a condo for high-rise gophers: the private offices are rodent-sized, the halls just wide enough for two-way pedestrianism.

You navigate the linoleum to the Department of Factual Verification. Directly across the hall is Clara's office, the door of which is almost always open so that all who come and go from the kingdom of facts must pass her scrutiny. She is torn between her desire for privacy, with all the honors, privileges, et cetera, appertaining to her post, and her desire to keep a sharp eye on her domain.

The door is wide open this morning and you can do nothing but make the sign of the cross and walk past. You sneak a glance over your shoulder as you enter the department and see that she's not at her desk. Your colleagues are all in place, except for Phoebe Hubbard, who is in Woods Hole researching a three-part piece on lobster-ranching.

"Good morning, fellow proles," you say, slipping into your seat. The Department of Factual Verification is the largest room in the magazine. If chess teams had locker rooms they might look like this. There are six desks—one reserved for visiting writers—and thousands of reference books on the walls. Gray linoleum desktops, brown linoleum floors. An absolute hierarchy is reflected in the desk assignments, with the desk farthest from Clara's office and closest to the windows reserved for the senior verificationist, and so on down to your own desk against the bookshelves next to the door—but in general the department is a clubhouse of democratic fellowship. The fanatic loyalty to the magazine which rules elsewhere is compromised here by a sense of departmental loyalty: us against them. If an error slips into the magazine, it is one of you, and not the writer, who will be crucified. Not fired, but scolded, perhaps even demoted to the messenger room or the typing pool.

Rittenhouse, who has served notice to falsehoods and commended facts for over fourteen years, nods and says good morning. He looks worried. You assume that Clingfast has been looking for you, that the notion of last straws has been aired.

"Has the Clinger been around yet," you ask. He nods and blushes down to his bow tie. Rittenhouse enjoys a touch of irreverence but can't help feeling guilty about it.

"She's rather perturbed," he says. "At least it seemed so to me," he adds, demonstrating the scruples of his profession. For half of his life this man has been reading some of the better liter-

ature and journalism of his time with the sole aim
of sorting out matters of fact from matters of opinion, disregarding the latter, and tracking the al-
leged facts through dusty volumes, along skeins
of microfilm, across transcontinental telephone
cables, till they prove good or are exposed as
error. He is a world-class detective, but his ded-
ication makes him wary of speech, as if a fiery
Clara Tillinghast stood guard on his larynx, ready
to pounce on the unqualified assertion.

Your nearest neighbor, Yasu Wade, is checking
a science piece. This is a mark of favor—Clingfast
usually reserving the science articles, the factual
verification of which is so urgent and satisfying,
for herself. Wade is on the phone. "Okay now,"
he says, "where does the neutrino fit into all of
this?" Wade grew up on Air Force bases until he
escaped to Bennington and New York. His speech
is Sunbelt Swish—a lisp on a twang, occasionally
supplemented by feigned R and L confusion, particularly when he has a chance to use the phrase
"President-elect." His mother is Japanese, his
father an Air Force captain out of Houston. They
married in Tokyo during the Occupation, and
Yasu Wade is the unlikely result. He calls himself
the *Yellow Nonpareil*. Wade is irreverent in every
direction, yet somehow manages to amuse where

you offend. He is Clara's favorite, not counting Rittenhouse, who is so naturally adapted to his environment as to be invisible.

"Tardy, very tardy," Wade says to you when he hangs up the phone. "This won't do. Facts wait for no man. Tardiness is a species of error with regard to Greenwich Mean Time. Greenwich Mean Time is now fifteen-fifteen hours, which means that Eastern Daylight Saving Time, which many of us observe hereabouts, is eleven-fifteen. Starting time here at the office is ten A.M.—hence an error in your disfavor of one hour and fifteen minutes."

In fact, things are more casual than Wade would have it: Clingfast likes to assert her prerogatives by coming in somewhere between ten-fifteen and ten-thirty. As long as one is at one's desk by ten-thirty, one is relatively safe. Somehow you manage to miss this banker's deadline at least once a week.

"Is she pissed," you ask.

"I wouldn't put it that way," Wade says. "I like that word better the way the British use it—colloquial for intoxicated: e.g., Malcolm Lowry's consul getting pissed on mescal in Quauhnahuac, if I remember the name of the town correctly."

"Can you spell it," you ask.

"Of course. But to return to your original question—yes, Clara is a tad peeved. She is not pleased with you. Or perhaps she is pleased to see you confirming her worst expectations. I think she's got the scent of blood. If I were you . . ." Wade looks toward the door and raises his eyebrows. "If I were you, I'd turn around."

Clingfast is in the door, looking like a good candidate for a Walker Evans Depression-era photo; flinty faced and suspicious. The guardian of the apertures, the priestess of Webster's Second Edition *Unabridged Dictionary*, eagle eyes and beagle nose. She gives you a look that could break glass, and then steps out. She's going to let you suffer for a while.

You dig into your desk and pull out a Vicks inhaler. Try to plow a path through some of the crusted snow in your head.

"Still got that nasty sinus problem, I see." Wade gives you a knowing look. Though he prides himself on being hip, he is too fastidious to do anything dangerous or dirty. You suspect that his sexual orientation is largely theoretical. He'd take a hot piece of gossip over a warm piece of ass any day of the week. He's always telling you who's sleeping with whom. Not that you mind. Last week it was David Bowie and Prince Rainier.

You try to settle down to an article about the French elections. It is your job to make sure that there are no errors of fact or spelling. In this case the facts are so confused as to suck you deep into vast regions of interpretation. The writer, a former restaurant critic, lavishes all his care on adjectives and disdains nouns. He describes an aging cabinet minister as "nubbly" and a rising socialist as "lightly browned." You believe that Clingfast gave you this piece in order to see you hang yourself. She knew the piece was a mess. She probably also knew that the claim of fluency in French on your résumé was something of a whopper, and that you are too proud to admit it now. Running down the facts requires numerous phone calls to France, and you made a fool of yourself last week doing your *je ne comprends pas* with various sub-ministers and their assistants. Plus you have your own personal reasons for not wanting to call Paris or speak French or be reminded of the goddamned place. Reasons that have to do with your wife.

There is no way you will be able to get everything in this article verified, and there is also no graceful way to admit failure. You are going to have to hope that the writer got some of it straight the first time, and that Clingfast doesn't go through the proofs with her usual razor-tooth comb.

Why does she hate you? She hired you, after all. When did things start to go wrong? It's not your fault that she never married. Since your own marital Pearl Harbor, you have understood that sleeping alone goes a long way toward explaining nastiness and erratic behavior. Sometimes you have wanted to tell her: *Hey, I know what it's like.* You have seen her at that little piano bar off Columbus, clutching her drink and waiting for somebody to come up and say hello. When she's bitching you out, you have wanted to say: *Why don't you just admit you hurt?* But by the time you understood this it was too late. She wanted your hide.

Maybe it all began with the John Donlevy deal. You had been at the magazine only a few weeks and Clara took a week off. Donlevy was doing a book review for the magazine, flexing his synapses after his second Pulitzer Prize. Book reviews were considered walk-throughs in the department, and Clara left the piece in your hands. In your innocence you not only fixed up the occasional citation error; you went on to suggest some improvements in the prose and to register questions regarding interpretation of the book. You handed in the proofs and went home well pleased. Something happened in Collating; your proofs were sent to Donlevy in place of the editor's proofs. The editor, a youngish woman fresh from the Yale alumni magazine, was in awe of her sudden proximity to Donlevy, and was horrified when she learned what had happened and looked over your proofs. You were summoned to her office and upbraided for your unprecedented presumption. To tamper with the prose of John Donlevy! Horrible. Un*think*able. You, a mere stripling of a verificationist. If you had gone to Yale, you might have learned some manners. She was trying to decide how best to explain the outrage to Donlevy when he called to say that he appreciated the suggestions and that he was taking several of the changes. You got that part of the story from the switchboard operator, who listened in on the conversation. The editor never spoke to you again. After Clara returned, there was another lecture, much the same, with the addition of the idea that you had embarrassed her and the entire department. When the issue came out, you noted with some satisfaction that your best stuff was incorporated in the review. But it was the end of Clara's warm maternal act.

To give Clara her due, lately you have not been impeccable in the performance of your duties. It's a matter of temperaments. You try and you try, but you can't see this as God's work, or even Man's work. Aren't computers supposed to free us from this kind of drudgery?

In fact, you don't want to be in Fact. You'd

much rather be in Fiction. You have cautiously expressed this preference several times, but there hasn't been an opening in Fiction in years. The people in the Verification Department tend to look down on fiction, in which words masquerade as flesh without the backbone of fact. There is a general sense that if fiction isn't dead, it is at least beside the point. But you'll take a new story by Bellow over a six-part article on the Republican convention at the drop of a hat. All the magazine fiction passes through the department, and since no one else wants it you take it upon yourself to do the routine checking—make sure that if a story set in San Francisco contains a psycho named Phil Doaks, there is no Phil Doaks in the San Francisco phone book who might turn around and sue. It's the opposite of verifying a factual piece. To confirm that the story doesn't unintentionally coincide at any point with real people and events. A cursory process, it does give you a shot at some decent reading. At first Clingfast seemed pleased that you were taking on a job no one else wanted, but now she accuses you of spending too much time on the fiction. You are an idler in the kingdom of facts. Meanwhile, the Fiction people are none too thrilled when you inform them that a story which contains a fly-fishing scene incorrectly has a hatch of Sulfur

Duns occurring on a stream in Oregon where, in fact, no Sulfur Duns have ever hatched. You are an unwilling emissary from the land of pedantry. "So what the hell does hatch in goddamned Oregon?" the editor asks. "Salmonflies, for one," you say. You want to say: It's my job—I don't like it either.

Megan Avery comes over to your desk. She picks up the framed needlepoint sampler Wade embroidered for your last birthday, which reads:

> Facts all come with points of view
> Facts don't do what I want them to.
> —TALKING HEADS

When Wade gave it to you you weren't sure whether to be grateful for his time and effort or insulted by the implied comment on your professional incapacities. Megan asks, "How's everything going with you?" You say you can't complain. "Are you sure?" Megan makes honesty seem like a viable alternative. She is a person who could give lessons in sanity. Why have you never confided in her before? She's older and wiser. You're not sure how old; she doesn't seem to have a particular age. You would describe her as striking, or attractive, but she has such an earnest, practical nature that it is hard for you to envision her as a sexual being. Although married once, she seems the West Village type meant to run her own life and help her friends through their many disasters. You admire her. You don't know many sensible people. Maybe you could have lunch sometime.

"I'm okay, really," you say.

"Need any help with the French piece? I'm not real busy just now."

"I think I can manage. Thanks."

The Clinger appears in the doorway. She nods at you. "We've decided to move the French thing up an issue. That means I need it on my desk before you leave today. We're closing tomorrow afternoon." She pauses. "Can you handle it?"

There is not a snowball's chance in hell and you suspect she knows it. "I could just give it directly to Collating tonight and save you the trouble."

"My desk," she says. "Tell me now if you're going to need help."

You shake your head. If she sees the shape the page proofs are in at the moment, you're screwed. You have not followed procedure. You have used pen where you should have used pencil, red pencil where you should have used blue. Phone numbers written in the margins, coffee rings in the columns. You have done all the things that the "Manual of Factual Verification" tells you not to do. You've got to try and find a clean copy of the proofs to work from. The Clinger is large on procedure.

The prospect of the work in front of you resurrects the unspeakable headache with which you woke. You're already exhausted. You're so tired. Eight days of sleep would put you right. A boatload of Marching Powder might get you through this ordeal. But simply to face it seems like more than you can do. You should protest the change in scheduling. Why the hell didn't someone ask you if it was almost ready to go? Even if you could speak French, it would take several more days. If you were not afraid of having Clara or the Druid examine your proofs as they stand, you would protest.

If you were Japanese, this would be the time to commit *seppuku*. Pen a farewell poem about the transience of cherry blossoms and the fleet transit of youth, wrap the sword blade in white silk, plunge it home and pull upward, rightward through your intestines. And no whimpering or sour expressions, please. You learned all about the ritual while checking an article on Japan. But you lack that samurai resolution. You are the kind of guy who always hopes for a miracle at the last minute. Manhattan does not lie in an earthquake zone, but there is always the possibility of nuclear war. Short of that, nothing you can imagine would alter the publishing schedule.

At a little after noon the Druid tiptoes past the office on his way to lunch. Because you happen to be staring out the door at nothing in particular you catch his eyes, famously nearsighted. He bows formally. The Druid is elusive; one has to look very closely, and know what to look for, to see him at all. While you have never actually seen a Victorian clerk, you believe this is what one would look like. At the magazine, his temperamental reticence has been elevated to a principle. Fourth in a dynastic succession, he has run the show for twenty years. Trying to discover what he is thinking is the preoccupation of the entire staff. Nothing passes into the magazine without his enthusiastic approval and his own final edit. There is no arbitration and no explanation. It pains him that he requires a staff to assist him, but he is invariably polite. There is officially no second-in-command, because that would imply an eventual changing of the guard, and the Druid cannot imagine the magazine without himself. The Kremlin must be a lot like this. Perhaps because he suspects he is mortal, fiction that deals too directly with death is unwelcome here; most references to myopia are edited out. No detail is too minute for his attention.

The only direct contact you have had with the Druid was when he called you up one day to worry about the English usage of the President of the United States. You were checking a piece in which the President warned against *precipitous* action. The Druid felt that *precipitate* was the word the President was looking for. He asked you to call the White House and get approval for the change. You dutifully called the White House and tried to explain the importance of this distinction. You spent several hours on hold. Those who actually believed you were serious would not commit themselves. Others just cussed you out. Meanwhile, the magazine was going to press. The Druid called three times and encouraged you to keep trying. Finally, with the composing room screaming for the final pages, an accommodation of sorts was reached, unknown to the President and his staff. While Webster's Second distinguished the meanings of the two words, the racier Third Edition listed them as synonyms. The Druid gave you a final call to explain this and to approve—not without trepidation—the original quote. The magazine went to press. Government continued apace.

❑

At one o'clock you go out for a sandwich. Megan asks you to bring her a Tab. Downstairs you semi-revolve through the doors and think about how nice it would be not to have to return at all, ever. You also think about how nice it would be to hole up in the nearest bar. The glare from the sidewalk stuns you; you fumble in your jacket pocket for your shades. Sensitive eyes, you tell people.

You shuffle off to the deli and pick up a pastrami-on-rye and an egg cream. The bald man behind the counter whistles cheerfully as he slices the meat. "Nice and lean today," he says. "And now for a little mustard—just how your mom used to make it."

"What do you know about it," you ask.

"Just passing the time, pal," he says, wrapping it all up. All of this, the dead meat on ice behind glass, everything, puts you off your meal.

Outside, waiting for a light, you are accosted by a man leaning up against a bank.

"My man, check it out here. Genuine Cartier

watches. Forty dollars. Wear the watch that'll make 'em watch you. The genuine article. Only forty bucks."

The man stands beside the torso of a mannequin, the arms of which are covered with watches. He holds one out to you. "Check it out." If you take it, you'll feel committed. But you don't want to be rude. You take the watch and examine it.

"How do I know it's real?"

"How do you know anything's real? Says *Cartier* right there on the face, right? Looks real. Feels real. So what's to know? Forty bucks. How can you lose?"

It appears authentic. Slim, rectangular face, regal roman numerals, sapphire-tipped winding knob. The band feels like good leather. But if it's real, it's probably hot. And if it isn't hot it can't be real.

"Thirty-five bucks to you. My cost."

"How come so cheap?"

"Low overhead."

You haven't owned a watch in years. Knowing the time at any given moment might be a good first step toward organizing the slippery flux of your life. You've never been able to see yourself as the digital kind of guy. But you could use a little Cartier in your act. It looks real, even if it isn't, and it tells time. What the hell.

"Thirty dollars," the man says.

"I'll buy it."

"At that price you ain't buying it. You're stealing it."

You wind your new watch and admire it on your wrist. 1:25.

Once you reach the office you realize you have forgotten Megan's Tab. You apologize and tell her you'll go back for it. She says not to bother. While you were gone she took two messages, one from Monsieur Somebody at the Department of Something, and one from your brother Michael. You don't really want to talk to either of them.

By two o'clock it's eight in Paris and everyone has gone home for the day. For the rest of the afternoon you will try to fill in the holes with reference books and calls to the consulate in New York. Your eyelids feel as if they are being held open by taxidermy needles. You push on blindly.

Your new watch dies at three-fifteen. You shake it, then wind it. The winding knob falls off in your hand.

The editor of the piece calls to ask how it's going. You say it's going. He apologizes for the scheduling change; he wanted to save it till next month at the earliest. For no clear reason, the Druid moved it up. "I just wanted to warn you," he says. "Take nothing for granted."

"That's my job," you say.

"I mean especially in this case. He hasn't left Paris in twelve years, and spends most of his time in restaurants. He never double-checks anything."

Jesus wept.

❑

Twice during the afternoon you call the writer to ask him where he picked up his facts. The first time you call you go through a list of errors and he concedes each point cheerfully.

"Where did you get this about the French government owning a controlling interest in Paramount Pictures?" you say.

"Don't they? Well, shit. Run a line through that."

"Your next three paragraphs depend on it."

"Damn. Who told me that?"

By the end of the second call he is annoyed, as if the errors were of your devising. This is the way it goes with the writers: they resent you to the degree that they depend on you.

Late in the afternoon a memo arrives addressed to "staff." It is signed by the Druid's assistant, which makes it gospel.

> It has come to our attention that a Mr. Richard Fox is writing an article about the magazine. Some of you may already have been approached by Mr. Fox. We have reason to believe that the intentions of this reporter are not coincident with the best interests of the magazine. We would like to remind all staff members of the magazine's policy with regard to the press. All queries and requests for interviews should be referred to this office. Under no circumstances should any employee presume to speak for the magazine without prior clearance. We remind you that all magazine business is strictly confidential.

The memo occasions amusement in the Department of Factual Verification. The magazine has been involved in many freedom of press trials, but in this gag order there is not a glimmer of irony.

Wade says, "I wish Richard Fox would call me."

Megan says, "Forget it, Yasu. I know for a fact that Richard Fox is straight."

"For a *fact*? I'd be very interested to hear about your verification procedure."

"I know you would," Megan says.

"At any rate," Wade says, "I only meant that I would be fantastically curious to know how many pieces of silver some of the institutional dirty laundry is worth. But don't get me wrong—it's not that I don't find Fox attractive."

Rittenhouse is tugging at his glasses, indicating that he wishes to speak. "I, for one, do not feel that Richard Fox is an objective reporter. He has a penchant for sensationalism."

"Of course," Wade says. "That's why we love him."

The possession of dangerous information excites a brief feeling of power here in the Department of Factual Verification. You wish Richard Fox or anyone else cared enough about Clara Tillinghast to perform a character assassination.

By seven everyone is gone. They all offered to help, and you waved them away. There is a shabby nobility in failing all by yourself.

Clara sticks her head in the door as she's leaving. "My desk," she says.

My ass, you think.

You nod and, in token of your earnestness, hunker down over the page proofs. From this point on it's a matter of covering your tracks, running pencil lines through anything that you have not been able to verify and hoping that nothing important slips through.

At seven-thirty Allagash calls. "What are you doing at the office?" he says. "We have plans for the evening. Monstrous events are scheduled."

Two of the things you like about Allagash are that he never asks you how you are and he never waits for you to answer his questions. You used to dislike this, but when the news is all bad it's a relief that someone doesn't want to hear it. Just now you want to stay at the surface of things, and Tad is a figure skater who never considers the sharks under the ice. You have friends who actually care about you and speak the language of the inner self. You have avoided them of late. Your soul is as disheveled as your apartment, and until you can clean it up a little you don't want to invite anyone inside.

Allagash tells you that Natalie and Inge are dying to meet you. Natalie's father runs an oil company and Inge is soon to be in a major television commercial. Moreover, the Deconstructionists are playing the Ritz, one of the modeling agencies is sponsoring a bash for Muscular Dystrophy at Magique and Natalie has cornered a chunk of the Gross National Product of Bolivia.

"I'm going to be working most of the night," you say. Actually, you are about to give up, but a night of Allagash is not the remedy for your blues. You're thinking of bed. You are so tired you could stretch out right here on the linoleum and slip into a long coma.

"Give me a time. I'll pick you up," Tad says.

The phrase "last-ditch effort" jumps out from the column of print in front of you. It makes you ashamed of yourself. You think of the Greeks at Thermopylae, the Texans at the Alamo, John Paul Jones in his leaky tub. You want to rally and whip hell out of falsehood and error.

You tell Tad you will call him back in half an hour. Later, when the phone rings, you ignore it.

At a little after ten you put the proofs on Clara's desk. It would at least be a relief if you could tell yourself that this was your best shot. You feel like a student who is handing in a term paper that is part plagiarism, part nonsense and half finished. You have scoped out and fixed a number of colossal blunders, which serves only to make you more aware of the suspect nature of everything you haven't verified. The writer was counting on the Verification Department to give authority to his sly observations and insidious generalizations. This is not cricket on his part, but it is your job to help him out and it is your job that is on the line. There has only been one printed retraction in the magazine's history and the verificationist responsible for the error was immediately farmed out to Advertising. Your only hope is that the Clinger won't read it. A fire of mysterious origin might sweep through the offices. Or Clara might get sloshed tonight, fall off a barstool and crack her head open. She might get picked up by a Sex Killer. Any *Post* reader will tell you it's possible. Happens every day.

There was a cartoon you used to watch, at least you think there was, with a time-traveling turtle and a benevolent wizard. The turtle would journey back to, say, the French Revolution, inevitably getting in way over his head. At the last minute, when he was stretched out under the guillotine, he would cry out, "Help, Mr. Wizard!" And the wizard, on the other end of the time warp, would wave his wand and rescue the hapless turtle.

Already you feel a sense of nostalgia as you walk down the narrow halls past all the closed doors. You remember how you felt when you passed this way for your first interview, how the bland seediness of the hallway only increased your apprehension of grandeur. You thought of all the names that had been made here. You thought of yourself in the third person: *He arrived for his first interview in a navy-blue blazer. He was interviewed for a position in the Department of Factual Verification, a job which must have seemed even then to be singularly unsuited to his flamboyant temperament. But he was not to languish long among the facts.*

Those first months seem now to have been filled with promise. You were convinced of the importance of your job and of the inevitability of rising above it. You met people you had admired half your life. You got married. The Druid himself sent a note of congratulations. It was only a matter of time before they realized your talents were being wasted in Fact.

Something changed. Somewhere along the line you stopped accelerating.

Mrs. Bender, the senior grammarian, is working late. You say good night. She asks you about the French piece and you tell her it's finished.

"What a mess," she says. "It reads as if it was translated literally from the Chinese. These damn writers want us to do all their work for them."

You nod and smile. Her complaint is refreshing, like rain at the end of a muggy day. You linger in the doorway while she shakes her head and clicks her tongue.

"Going home soon?" you say.

"Not soon enough."

"Can I get you something from downstairs?"

She shakes her head. "I don't want to feel as if I'm settled in here."

"See you tomorrow."

She nods and returns to her proofs.

You walk to the elevator and press the Down button.

THE
UTILITY
OF
FICTION

You see yourself as the kind of guy who appreciates a quiet night at home with a good book. A little Mozart on the speakers, a cup of cocoa on the arm of the chair, slippers on the feet. Monday night. It feels like Thursday, at least. Walking from subway to apartment, you tell yourself that you are going to suppress this rising dread that comes upon you when you return home at night. A man's home, after all, is his castle. Approaching your building on West Twelfth Street, you observe the architect's dim concept of European fortresses: a crenelated tower atop the building conceals the water tank and the entrance is fitted with a mock portcullis. You let yourself in the front door and gingerly unlock the mailbox. No telling what might be inside. One of these days there could be a letter from Amanda explaining her desertion, begging forgiveness or asking you to send the rest of her stuff to a new address.

Tonight there is an overdue notice from VISA; a solicitation from Recording for the Blind; a letter from Jim Winthrop in Chicago, college roommate, best man at your wedding; and something corporate for Amanda White. You open Jim's letter first. It starts "Hey stranger," and ends with "regards to Amanda." The letter to Amanda is a printout on an insurance company letterhead, her name typed into the salutation:

> Let's face it—in your business, your face is your greatest asset. Modeling is an exciting and rewarding career. In all likelihood, you have many years of earning ahead of you. But where would you be in the event of a disfiguring accident? Even a minor injury could spell the end of a lucrative career and the loss of hundreds of thousands of dollars in potential income.

You ball up the letter and arc it into the waste-basket beside the elevator. You press the button. *Where would you be, for instance, if a spurned husband threw acid in your face?* No. Stop this. This is not your better self speaking. This is not how you feel.

The sound of the tumblers in the locks of your apartment door puts you in mind of dungeons. The place is haunted. Just this morning you found a makeup brush beside the toilet. Memories lurk like dustballs at the backs of drawers. The stereo is a special model that plays only music fraught with poignant associations.

This was the second apartment you shared with Amanda, the place into which you moved in order to accommodate the wedding gifts. Amanda wanted to live on the Upper East Side, where the other models lived. She brought home prospecti for co-ops and then, when you asked her where the money was going to come from, suggested you could get a loan from your father. You asked her what made her think that even if your father had that kind of money on hand, he would want to fork it over. She shrugged. "Anyway, I'm doing really well right now," she said. For the first time you realized that she thought your family was rich, and by the standards of her childhood they were. "Come look at this kitchen plan," she said.

This place was your compromise—an uptown sort of building downtown: high ceilings, daytime doorman, working fireplaces. You both liked the wood paneling and the wainscoting. Amanda said it was a place in which you would not feel ridiculous eating off the new china with the sterling flatware. Flatware, china and crystal occupied much of her concern as the wedding approached. She insisted that you buy a starter set of Tiffany sterling: the price of silver was going through the ceiling and she was convinced that it would double or triple by the time of the wedding. A famous designer told her so. With the earnings of three weeks' showroom work she bought six settings. A few days later silver collapsed, and the six settings were worth about what she paid for one.

When she heard you had a family crest she wanted to put it on the sterling, but you drew the line at your monograms and feared the sense of urgency in her new acquisitiveness. She seemed eager to provision you all at once for a lifetime. Then, within a year of this prenuptial buying spree, she was gone. Now you eat out of paper cartons and the wainscoting doesn't cheer you. What's more, you can't really afford the rent. You keep meaning to look for a new place, and to do the dishes and the laundry.

You close the door and stand in the foyer, listening. For some time after Amanda left, you would pause here in the hope that you would hear her inside, that she had returned, that you would discover her, penitent and tender, when you stepped into the living room. That hope is mostly gone, but still you observe this brief vigil inside the door, gauging the quality of the silence to see if it is only the melancholy silence of absence, or whether it is full of high-register shrieks and moans. Tonight you are uncertain. You step into the living room and throw your jacket on the love seat. You hunt up your slippers and read the spines of the books in the shelves, determined to make a go of this quiet-night-at-home idea. A random sampling of titles induces vertigo: *As I Lay Dying, Under the Volcano, Anna Karenina, Being and Time, The Brothers Karamazov.* You must have had an ambitious youth. Of course, many of these spines have never been cracked. You have been saving them up.

Nothing seems to be what you want to do until you consider writing. Suffering is supposed to be the raw stuff of art. You could write a book. You feel that if only you could make yourself sit down at a typewriter you could give shape to what seems merely a chain reaction of pointless disasters. Or you could get revenge, tell your side of the story, cast some version of yourself in the role of wronged hero. Hamlet on the battlements. Maybe get outside autobiography altogether, lose yourself in the purely formal imperatives of words in the correct and surprising sequence, or create a fantasy world of small furry and large scaly creatures.

You have always wanted to be a writer. Getting the job at the magazine was only your first step toward literary celebrity. You used to write what you believed to be urbane sketches infinitely superior to those appearing in the magazine every week. You sent them up to Fiction; they came back with polite notes. "Not quite right for us now, but thanks for letting us see this." You would try to interpret the notes: what about the word *now*—do they mean that you should submit this again, later? It wasn't the notes so much as the effort of writing that discouraged you. You never stopped thinking of yourself as a writer biding his time in the Department of Factual Verification. But between the job and the life there wasn't much time left over for emotion recollected in tranquillity. For a few weeks you got up at six to compose short stories at the kitchen table while

Amanda slept in the other room. Then your night life started getting more interesting and complicated, and climbing out of bed became harder and harder. You were gathering experience for a novel. You went to parties with writers, cultivated a writerly persona. You wanted to be Dylan Thomas without the paunch, F. Scott Fitzgerald without the crack-up. You wanted to skip over the dull grind of actual creation. After a hard day of work on other people's manuscripts—knowing in your heart that you could do better—the last thing you wanted to do was to go home and write. You wanted to go out. Amanda was the fashion model and you worked for the famous magazine. People were happy to meet you and to invite you to their parties. So much was going on. Of course, mentally, you were always taking notes. Saving it all up. Waiting for the day when you would sit down and write your masterpiece.

You dig your typewriter out of the closet and set it up on the dining-room table. You have some good twenty-pound bond from the supply cabinet in the office. You roll a sheet, with backing, onto the platen. The whiteness of the sheet is intimidating, so you type the date in the right-hand corner. You decide to jump immediately into the story you have in mind. Waste no time with preliminaries. You type:

He was expecting her on the afternoon flight from Paris when she called to say she would not be coming home.

"You're taking a later flight?" he asked.

"No," she said. "I'm starting a new life."

You read it over. Then you tear the sheet out of the typewriter and insert a new one.

Go farther back, maybe. Try to find the source of this chaos. Give her a name and a place.

Karen liked to look at her mother's fashion magazines. The women were elegant and beautiful and they were always climbing in and out of taxis and limousines on their way to big stores and restaurants. Karen didn't think there were any stores or restaurants like that in Oklahoma. She wished she looked like the ladies in the pictures. Then maybe her father would come back.

This is dreadful. You tear the sheet into eighths and slide them into the wastebasket. You insert another piece of paper; again you type the date. At the left margin you type, "Dear Amanda," but when you look at the paper it reads "Dead Amanda."

Screw this. You are not going to commit any

great literature tonight. You need to relax. After all, you've been busting ass all day. You check the fridge; no beer. A finger of vodka in the bottle on the sink. Maybe you will step out and get a six-pack. Or wander over to the Lion's Head, as long as you're going out, to see if there's anybody you know. It's not impossible there to meet a woman *avec* hair, *sans* tattoo, at the bar.

The intercom buzzes while you're changing your shirt. You push the Talk button: "Who is it?"

"Narcotics squad. We're soliciting donations for children all over the world who have no drugs."

You buzz him up. You're not sure how you feel about the advent of Tad Allagash. While you could use company, Tad can be too much of a good thing. His brand of R & R is nothing if not strenuous. Nonetheless, by the time he gets to the door, you're glad to see him. He's looking *très sportif* in J. Press torso and punked-out red SoHo trousers. He presents his hand and you shake.

"Ready to roll?"

"Where are we rolling?"

"Into the heart of the night. Wherever there are dances to be danced, drugs to be hoovered, women to be Allagashed. It's a dirty job but someone's got to do it. Speaking of drugs, are you in possession?"

You shake your head.

"Not a single line for young Tad?"

"Sorry."

"Not even a mirror I can lick?"

"Suit yourself."

Tad goes over to the mahogany-and-gilt-framed mirror that you inherited from your grandmother, the one Amanda was so afraid your cousin was going to nab. He runs his tongue over the glass.

"There's something on here."

"Dust."

Tad smacks his lips. "In this apartment the dust has better coke content than some of the shit we buy by the gram. All us coke fiends sneezing— it adds up."

Tad runs his finger across the length of the coffee table. "It looks like you could teach a course in dust here. Did you know that ninety percent of your average household dust is composed of human epidermal matter? That's skin, to you."

Perhaps this explains your sense of Amanda's omnipresence. She has left her skin behind.

He walks over to the table and leans over the typewriter. "Doing a little writing, are we? *Dead Amanda*. That's the idea. I told you you'd get more nookie than you can shake a stick at if you tell the girls that your wife died. It's the sympathy vote. More effective than saying she fit you with

57

horns and kited off to Paris. Avoid the awful taint of rejection."

Tad's first reaction, when you told him about Amanda's departure, contained a grain of genuine sympathy and regret. His second reaction was to tell you that you could make a fine erotic career for yourself by repeating the story just as you had told it to him, adding touches of pathos and cruel irony. Finally, he advised you to say that Amanda had died in a plane crash on her way home from Paris on the day of your first anniversary.

"You're sure there aren't any drugs around here?"

"Some Robitussin in the bathroom."

"I'm disappointed in you, Coach. I've always thought of you as the kind of guy who saves something for a rainy day. The temperate sort."

"I've fallen in with bad companions."

"Let's get on the phone," Tad says. "We must locate party fuel. *Cherchez les grammes.*"

All the people who might have drugs aren't home. The people who are home don't have drugs. There is a pattern here. "Damn Warner," Tad says. "He never answers his phone. I just know he's sitting there in his loft on top of a pile of toot, ignoring the phone." Tad hangs up and checks his watch, which tells him the time in selected major cities of the world, including New York

and Dubai, Persian Gulf, Oman. "Eleven-forty.
A little too early for Odeon, but once we're downtown, it's happy hunting ground for sneeze and
squeeze. Ready?"

"Have you ever experienced this nearly over-
whelming urge for a quiet night at home?"

Tad reflects for a moment. "No."

The glittering, curvilinear surfaces inside Odeon
are reassuring. The place makes you feel reasonable at any hour, often against bad odds, with its
good light and clean luncheonette-via-Cartier deco
decor. Along the bar are faces familiar under ar-
tificial light, belonging to people whose daytime
existence is only a tag—designer, writer, artist.
A model from Amanda's agency is sitting at the
bar. You do not want to see her. Tad cruises right
over and kisses her. At the other end of the bar
you order a vodka. You finish it and order a second before Tad beckons. The model is with another woman. Tad introduces them as Elaine and
Theresa. Elaine, the model, has a punk high-
fashion look: short, razor-cut dark hair, high
cheekbones, eyebrows plucked straight. Metallic
and masculine are the adjectives that come to
mind. Both M words. Theresa is blond, too short

and busty to model. Elaine looks you over as if you were an impulse purchase that she might return to the department store.

"Aren't you Amanda White's boyfriend?"

"Husband. I mean, I was."

"She was in Paris showing the fall collections," Tad says, "and she got caught in a crossfire between Palestinian terrorists and the French police. Totally fluke thing. Innocent bystander. Senseless death. He doesn't like to talk about it." Tad's delivery is entirely convincing. You almost believe him yourself. His air of being privy to dark secrets and inside stories gives credence to outrageous statements.

"That's terrible," Theresa says.

"Tragic is what it is," Tad says. "Excuse me, but I've got to do some business. Back in a minute." He bows and then heads out the door.

"Is that true?"

"Not really."

"What is Amanda doing these days," Elaine asks.

"I don't know. I think she's in Paris."

"Wait a minute," Theresa says. "Is she alive?"

"We just sort of split up."

"Too bad for you," Elaine says. "She was yummy." She turns to Theresa. "Sort of this slinky

girl-next-door look. Farm fresh. Very ingen-
uous."

"I don't understand this," Theresa says.

"Me neither," you say. You'd just as soon change
the subject. You don't like this role of bird with
broken wing, especially since that's exactly how
you feel. The lame-duck husband. You'd rather
be an eagle or a falcon, pitiless and predatory
among the solitary crags.

"Aren't you some kind of writer?" Elaine says.

"I do some writing. I'm sort of an editor actually."

"Oh, God," Theresa says, when you mention
the name of the magazine. "I've been reading it
all my life. I mean, my parents get it. I always
read it at the gynecologist. What's your name?
Should I know you?" She asks you about writers
and artists on the staff. You dish up a standard
portion of slander and libel that would never pass
the Clinger's requirements of verification.

Without getting too specific you imply that your
job is extremely demanding and important. In
the past you could often convince yourself as well
as others of this, but your heart is no longer in
it. You hate this posturing, even as you persist,
as if it were important for these two strangers to
admire you for all the wrong reasons. It's not

much, this menial job in a venerable institution, but it's all you've got left.

Once upon a time, you assumed you were very likable. That you had an attractive wife and a fairly interesting job seemed only your due. You were a good guy. You deserved some of the world's booty. After you met Amanda and came to New York, you began to feel that you were no longer on the outside looking in. When you were growing up you suspected that everyone else had been let in on some fundamental secret which was kept from you. Others seemed to know what they were doing. This conviction grew with each new school you attended. Your father's annual job transfers made you the perennial new kid. Every year there was a new body of lore to be mastered. The color of your bike, your socks, was always wrong. If you ever go into psychoanalysis, you will insist that the primal scene is not the encounter of parents in coitus: it takes the shape of a ring of schoolchildren, like Indians surrounding a wagon train, laughing with malice, pointing their vicious little fingers to insist upon your otherness. The scene repeated itself in schoolyards across the country. Not until you reached college, where everyone started fresh, did you begin to pick up the tricks of winning friends and influencing people. Although you became adept, you also felt that you were exercising an acquired skill, something that came naturally to others. You succeeded in faking everyone out, and never quite lost the fear that you would eventually be discovered a fraud, an impostor in the social circle. Which is just about how you feel these days. Even now, as you puff yourself up with tales of high adventure in magazine publishing, you can see Elaine's eyes wandering out over the room, leaving you behind. She's drinking champagne. As you watch, she dips her tongue into the tulip bowl and slides it around inside the glass.

A woman who looks vaguely famous glances up from her table and waves. Elaine waves back. Her smile goes sour when the woman turns away.

"Check that out," Elaine says. "Silicone implants."

"I don't know. She looks pretty damn flat to me."

"Not the tits—the cheeks. She's got fucking silicone implants to make it look like she has cheekbones."

Tad comes back, pleased with himself. "Bingo," he says.

It's somewhere past midnight. Anything that starts now is not going to end at a reasonable hour. You think about slipping out and heading home. All sorts of beneficial effects are rumored to accrue from a good night's sleep. On the other hand, you wouldn't mind a taste of that toot. Just enough to boost your morale.

In a moment you are all en route to the bathroom downstairs. Tad lays out some fat lines on the toilet seat. Elaine and Theresa take their turns. Finally, Tad hands you the bill. The sweet nasal burn hits like a swallow of cold beer on a hot August day. Tad fixes another round and by the time you all troop out of the bathroom you are feeling omnipotent. You are upwardly mobile. Certainly something excellent is bound to happen.

"Let us locomote out of here," Tad says.

"Where to?" Theresa says. "Where the boys are?"

"Where the girls are," Elaine says. You're not sure if this is just having fun with movie allusions or something more pointed.

Your merry band decides that Heartbreak is the destination. A cab is procured for the short hop uptown.

Outside the door there is a crowd of would-be Heartbreakers with a uniform outer-borough look. Tad pushes through the supplicants, confers with the bouncer and then waves the three of you in. Elaine and Theresa are chatting away when it comes time to pay, so you cover one and Tad covers the other. Inside, there is still room to move.

"It's early," Tad says. He is disappointed. He hates to arrive before everyone else is in place. He takes pride in his timing, being on time by being the latest.

Elaine and Theresa disappear and you don't see them for fifteen minutes. Tad discovers some friends, advertising people, at a table. Everyone is discussing the new *Vanity Fair*. Some are for and some against. "Utter confusion," says Steve, a copywriter. "It's the Abstract Expressionist approach to publishing. Throw ink at paper. Hope for pattern to emerge."

You go off to buy a drink, keeping both eyes peeled for lonely women. There don't seem to be any at the moment. Everyone knows everyone else. You are on the anti-cline of your first rush. You are also experiencing the inevitable disappointment of clubs. You enter with an anticipation that on the basis of past experience is entirely unjustified. You always seem to forget that you don't really like to dance. Since you are already here, though, you owe it to yourself to make a sustained assault on the citadel of good times. The music pumps you up, makes you want to do something, not necessarily dance. The drugs make you feel the music and the music makes you want to do more drugs.

At the bar someone thumps your shoulder. You turn around. It takes you a minute to place the face, but in the time it takes to shake hands you come up with a name: Rich Vanier. He was in your dining club at college. You ask what he's been doing. He's in banking, just back from South America tonight, after saving a banana republic from bankruptcy.

"What the hell, I restructured, gave the generals a few more months of high living. So what are you doing to keep body and soul together. Still the poet?"

"I do a little South American business myself."

"I heard a rumor you married an actress."

"*Activist*. I married a beautiful activist. She was the illegitimate daughter of Che Guevara. A few months ago she went home to visit her mother and got herself arrested and tortured by a series of rich South American generals. She died in prison."

"You're kidding, right?"

"Do I look like I'm kidding?"

Rich Vanier can't get away from you fast enough. He says you'll have to have lunch sometime.

Walking back to the table you see Theresa and

Elaine heading off with Tad. You catch up with them just outside the Men's Room. The four of you occupy a stall. Elaine sits on the tank and Theresa sits on the seat.

"Seems like I spend about half my life in bathrooms," Theresa says as she blocks off a nostril.

Later you run into a woman you met at a party. You can't remember her name. She acts embarrassed when you greet her, as if something shameful had once passed between you, though all you can remember is a discussion about the political ramifications of The Clash. You ask her if she wants to dance and she says sure.

Out on the floor, you invent your own dance step. You call it the New York Torque. "Some Girls" segues to "Shattered." You keep outstripping the prevailing tempo. Your partner sways back and forth metronomically. When you look at her, she seems to be studying you sympathetically. After you have soaked through your shirt you ask her if she wants to take a break. She nods her head vigorously.

"Is there something the matter?" You have to shout in her ear to be heard.

"Not really."

"You seem nervous."

"I heard about your wife," she says. "I'm so sorry."

"What did you hear?"

"About what happened. About the, you know, leukemia."

You are riding the Bolivian Local up through the small mountain villages into the lean oxygen of the Andean peaks.

"We've got Terrain and Elisa eating out of our hands," Tad says. "I think it's time we suggested that we all slip out to someplace more comfortable."

You are in the bathroom again. Elaine and Theresa are in the Ladies' on legitimate business.

"I do not appreciate this leukemia bit," you say. "Not funny."

"Just trying to boost sales. Consider me your agent."

"I'm not amused. Bad taste."

"Taste," says Tad, "is a matter of taste."

You are dancing with Elaine. Tad is dancing with Theresa. Elaine moves with an angular syncopation that puts you in mind of the figures on Egyptian tombs. It may be a major new dance step. Whatever it is, she is making you feel self-conscious. She's a tough act to accompany. You feel like a recent transplant from the junior prom. You are not particularly attracted to Elaine, who's too hard-edged in your view. You do not even think she is a particularly nice person. Yet you have this desire to prove that you can have as good a time as anyone, that you can be one of the crowd. Objectively, you know that Elaine is desirable, and you feel obligated to desire her. It seems to be your duty to go through the motions. You keep thinking that with practice you will eventually get the knack of enjoying superficial encounters, that you will stop looking for the universal solvent, stop grieving. You will learn to compound happiness out of small increments of mindless pleasure.

"I really enjoyed Amanda," Elaine says between songs. "I do hope I see her again." There is something confidential in her manner, as if you shared a secret with regard to Amanda. You would be happier if she had said she didn't like Amanda. Being still unable to think the worst of her, you need other people to think it and speak it for you.

Tad and Theresa have disappeared. Elaine excuses herself and says she will be right back. You feel abandoned. You consider the possibility of conspiracy. They have planned to meet at the door and ditch you. You are doing bad things to their mood. Or, worse yet, you are missing out on drugs. You get yourself a drink. You wait five minutes and then decide to reconnoiter. You check the Men's Room first and then the Ladies'. A woman in a leather jump suit is teasing her hair at the mirror. "Plenty of room," she says. You hear sounds coming from one of the stalls. Giggling. Looking down, you see Elaine's pumps and Theresa's sandals under the door.

"Save a little for me," you say, pushing on the door of the stall, which yields just enough to allow you to stick your head in and discover Elaine and Theresa engaged in an unnatural act. You look on in wonder and confusion.

"Want to join the party?" Elaine asks.

"*Bon appétit*," you blurt, and you lurch out of the Ladies' Room. You emerge into a din of bodies and music.

It is very late.

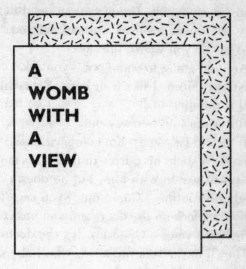

A
WOMB
WITH
A
VIEW

You dream about the Coma Baby. You sneak into the hospital, past the nurses and reporters. Nobody can see you. A door with a plaque reading *L'Enfant Coma* opens into the Department of Factual Verification. Elaine and Amanda are doing lines on Yasu Wade's desk and swearing in French. The Coma Mom is stretched out on your desk in a white gown. IV bottles are hanging from the bookshelves, tubes plugged into her arms. The gown is open around her midsection. You approach and discover that her belly is a transparent bubble. Inside you can see the Coma Baby. He opens his eyes and looks at you.

"What do you want?" he says.

"Are you going to come out," you ask.

"No way, José. I like it in here. Everything I need is pumped in."

"But Mom's on her way out."

"If the old lady goes, I'm going with her." The Coma Baby sticks his purple thumb in his mouth. You try to reason with him, but he does a deaf-and-dumb routine. "Come out," you say. Then there is a knock on the door, and you hear Clara Tillinghast's voice: "Open up. It's the doctor."

"They'll never take me alive," the Baby says.

The phone is ringing. The receiver squirts out of your hand like a trout. You keep expecting things to be solid and they're not. You recover the receiver from the floor and apply it to your face. One end goes next to your ear and the other next to your mouth.

"*Allô?*" You expect the speaker to be French. It's Megan Avery. She wanted to make sure you were awake. Oh yes, you were just making some breakfast. Sausage and eggs.

"I hope you don't mind," she says. "But I didn't want you getting in Dutch with Clara again. I thought I'd just make sure you were awake." *In Dutch?* You make a note to look up this expression in Partridge's dictionary of slang when you get to work. The clock says nine-fifteen. You slept through the eight-thirty alarm. You thank Meg and tell her you will see her at work.

"You're sure you're awake?" she says.

It certainly feels like it: headache, sour stomach—all the vital signs.

The generalized dread attendant upon regaining consciousness becomes localized around the image of Clara Tillinghast. You can face the fact that you will probably lose your job, but you do not think you can face Clara. Not on four hours of teeth-grinding sleep. Nor can you stand the sight of those page proofs—the evidence of your failure. In your dreams you have been on the phone to Paris, waiting for the piece of information that would save your life. You were barricaded inside the Department of Factual Verification. Someone was pounding the door. You were holding the line. The operator broke in intermittently, speaking in a language you could not even partly understand. The palms of your hands have been flayed by your fingernails. All night you lay with your arms held rigidly at your sides, your fists clenched.

73

You consider calling in sick. She would call up sometime during the day to say you were fired and you could hang up before she got abusive. But the magazine goes to press tomorrow and your absence would put pressure on your colleagues. And hiding would rob your failure of dignity. You think of Socrates, the kind of guy who accepted his cup and drank it down. More than this, you cling to the hope that you will somehow escape your fate.

You're dressed and out of the house before ten. The train pulls in just as you make the platform. You consider letting it go by. You're not quite ready yet. You need to hone the steel of your resolution, consider your strategy. The doors close with a pneumatic hiss. But someone in the back is holding one open for a man who is running up the platform. The doors open again. You step onto the train. The car is full of Hasidim from Brooklyn—gnomes in black with briefcases full of diamonds. You take a seat beside one of them. He is reading from his Talmud, running his finger across the page. The strange script is similar to the graffiti signatures all over the surfaces of the subway car, but the man does not look up at the graffiti, nor does he try to steal a peek at the headlines of your *Post*. This man has a God and a History, a Community. He has a perfect econ-

omy of belief in which pain and loss are explained
in terms of a transcendental balance sheet, in
which everything works out in the end and death
is not really death. Wearing black wool all summer must seem like a small price to pay. He
believes he is one of God's chosen, whereas you
feel like an integer in a random series of numbers.
Still, what a fucking haircut.

At Fourteenth Street three Rastafarians get on,
and soon the car reeks of sweat and reefer. Sometimes you feel like the only man in the city without group affiliation. An old lady with a Macy's
bag sitting across from you looks around as if to
ask what the world is coming to between these
Dracula Jews and zonked-out Africans, but when
you smile at her she quickly looks away. You
could start your own group—the Brotherhood of
Unfulfilled Early Promise.

The *Post* confirms your sense of impending
disaster. There's a Fiery Nightmare on page
three—an apartment blaze in Queens; and on
page four a Killer Tornado that ravaged Nebraska. In the heartland of the country, carnage
is usually the result of acts of God. In the city
it's manmade—arson, rape, murder. Anything
that goes wrong in other parts of the world can
usually be attributed to the brutishness of foreigners. It's a nice, simple world view. The Coma

Baby is buried on page five. No developments: COMA BABY LIVES. The doctors are considering a premature Caesarean delivery.

It's ten-ten when you come up on Times Square, ten-sixteen when you enter the building. The first elevator down is operated by a kid who looks like his last job was purse snatching. You say good morning and step into the back. After a minute he turns around.

"You gonna tell me what floor or do I gotta be psychic?"

You tell him twenty-nine. Accustomed to Lucio and his gracious peers, this kid strikes you as a rude interloper. He swings the gate closed and latches the door. Halfway up he takes out a Vicks inhaler and snorts on it. This makes your nose twitch sympathetically.

"Twenty-nine," he says when you get to the floor. "Ladies' undies and accessories."

No armed guards waiting for you. You ask Sally, the receptionist, if Clara is in yet.

"Not yet," she says. You're not sure if this is good news or bad. It could be a case of prolonging the agony. Your colleagues are all huddled around a copy of the *New York Times*, the newspaper of record and of choice here in Fact. Clara told you when you were hired that all members of the department were expected to read the paper thoroughly, excluding the new features sections, but you haven't looked at it in weeks.

"Is it war," you ask.

Rittenhouse tells you that one of the magazine's writers, a favorite among members of the Department for her scrupulous research and general lack of snottiness toward underlings, has just won a big award for her series on cancer research. *Cancer*. Rittenhouse is particularly pleased because he helped research the articles. "How about that?" he says. He holds up the paper so you can see the article. You are about to nod your head and impersonate enthusiasm when you see the ad on the facing page. You take the paper from Rittenhouse. There are three women modeling cocktail dresses and one of them is Amanda. You feel dizzy. You sit back on the desk and look at the picture. It's Amanda, all right. You didn't even know she was in New York. The last you heard she was in Paris and planning to stay. She might have had the decency to call as long as she's here. But, then, what is there to say?

Why does she have to haunt you like this? If she would just work in an office like everyone else. Right before she left she mentioned a billboard contract, and you have dreamt of seeing her face, monstrously enlarged, on the wall across from your apartment.

"I think we can all be proud of her," Ritten-house says.

"What?"

"Is anything wrong," Meg asks.

You shake your head and fold up the paper. *Leukemia, Tad said.* Meg tells you that Clara hasn't come in yet. You thank her for the wake-up call. Wade asks if you finished the French piece and you say, "More or less."

On the first Tuesday of the month, everyone gets one of the short pieces from the front section of the magazine. The articles have already been divvied up: yours is a report on the annual meeting and reception of The Polar Explorers Society, held this year at the Sherry Netherland. The Polar Explorers are predictably eccentric. They wear divers' watches and obscure military decorations. The hors d'oeuvres at the reception include blubber and smoked Emperor Penguin on Triscuits. You underline *Emperor Penguin* and make a note to check the spelling and whether or not it is edible. Also check spelling on *Triscuits*. As Clara says, one can't be too careful. If you botch a brand name the manufacturer will never let you hear the end of it. If there were no such thing as an Emperor Penguin, or if it were an Empress, three hundred letters would land in the mailroom by the middle of next week. The magazine's most fanatic readers are exactly the sort who would know about penguins; ornithology seems to be a particular field of scrutiny, and the slightest error or even vagueness of fact brings a flurry of vigilant correspondence. Just last month an innocuous sketch on birdfeeder activity raised a storm. Readers protested that a certain type of finch couldn't possibly have been at a feeder in Stonington, Connecticut, when the writer claimed to have seen a pair. The letters are still coming in. The Druid called Meg, who worked on the piece, and asked for the opinion of the Audubon Society. The matter is still under advisement. You once wrote a spoof on this genre called "Birds of Manhattan," which amused your colleagues but disappeared without a trace when you sent it upstairs to Fiction.

First stop on the present assignment is volume E for Emperor of the *Encyclopaedia Britannica*. No sign of penguins, but there's a fascinating article about embryology with sequential pix of the human egg changing from a salamander at ten days into a homunculus at ten weeks. Eventually you replace E on the shelf and reach for P, one of your favorites. *Paralysis; Paranoid Reactions; Parasitology*, for fun and profit, subchapters on rhizopods, ciliates, flagellates and sporozoans. *Pardubice*, a town in the East Bohemian section of Czechoslovakia, an important junction on the Brno-Prague line. *Paris*, with color pix; *Particles*, *Elementary*; *Pascal*; *Pavlov*; *Peccary*, the New World counterpart of the swine (w. pic.); *Pedro*, the name of five kings of Portugal. Finally, *Penguins*. Flightless and clumsy on land. You know the feeling. The Emperor reaches a height of four feet. No mention of edibility. In the picture they look like eccentric Polar Explorers dressed for a reception at the Sherry Netherland.

Your colleagues are abuzz with details from their own pieces. Wade has one about an inventor who has just received his hundredth patent, for a rotary nose-hair clipping device. Wade gets the inventor on the phone and learns that he was also responsible for the automatic toilet-bowl cleaning revolution, although the big companies stole the idea out from under him and made millions. He gives Wade a long account of this injustice and then says he can't discuss the matter because it's under litigation. All this should be wonderfully diverting, yet there is a forced quality to your laughter. You find it hard to listen to what other people are saying, or to understand the words of the article on which you are ostensibly working. You read the same paragraph over and over, trying to remember the difference between a matter of fact and a matter of opinion. Should you call up the president of the Polar Explorers and ask if it's true that someone was wearing a headdress made out of walrus skin? Does it matter? And why does the spelling of *Triscuit* look so strange? You keep watching the door for Clara. Odd phrases of French run through your brain.

The first thing to do is call the writer and get from him the number of someone who can confirm that such a society exists, that it had a reception at the hotel mentioned, on the date mentioned, that this is a matter of fact and not fiction. Names are named. You must find out if these names belong to real people and, if so, how they are spelled.

Rittenhouse announces that he's just had a call from Clara, who is sick and won't be in: the reprieve you have been waiting for. The boa constrictor wrapped around your heart eases its grip. Who knows? The illness might prove serious.

"Actually," Rittenhouse continues, "what she said is that she would not be in *this morning*. She's not certain if she will be feeling well enough to come in this afternoon. She can't say at this point." He pauses and tugs on his glasses, con-

sidering whether further qualification is necessary, and then concludes, "Anyone wishing to
consult her may call her at home."

You ask Rittenhouse if there are any messages.

"Nothing specific," he answers.

Here is your chance to redeem yourself. A
day's work might pull you into the clear with the
French piece. You could get the guys in Typesetting to cut you a few hours' slack on the deadline. You could get the Penguin thing out of the
way in half an hour and then buckle down to it.

Alors! Vite, vite! Allons-y!

An hour later, the Polar Explorers are put to bed.
It's a little after noon, and your energy is flagging.
What you need is some lunch to set you right.
Return to the French elections with renewed vigor.
Maybe pick up *une baguette* with ham and Brie
to get you into the proper frame of mind. You
ask if anybody wants anything from the outer
world. Megan gives you money for a bagel

On the way out you see Alex Hardy standing
in front of the water cooler staring into the aqua-
marine glass. He looks up, startled, and then,
seeing it's only you, he says hello. He turns back

to the water cooler and says, "I was just thinking it could use some fish."

Alex is a Fiction Editor Emeritus, a relic from the early days, a man who speaks of the venerable founders by their nicknames. He started out as an office boy, made his rep as a writer of satiric sketches of Manhattan high life that abruptly stopped appearing for reasons which are still the subject of speculation, and became an editor. He discovered and encouraged some of the writers you grew up on, but he has not discovered anybody in years and his main function seems to be as the totem figure of Continuity and Tradition. Only one story has emerged from his office in the time you have been on the staff. No one can say whether his drinking is a function of his decline or whether it is the other way around. You expect cause and effect are inextricable in these cases. Mornings he is thoughtful and witty, if somewhat ravaged. In the afternoons he sometimes wanders down to the Department of Factual Verification and waxes nostalgic. You believe he likes you, insofar as he likes anyone. He attached detailed memos to several of your short-story submissions, critiques both blunt and encouraging. He took your work seriously, although the fact that it ended up on his desk was perhaps an indication that it was not taken seriously in the Department of Fiction. You are fond of this man. While others view him as a sunken ship, you have a fantasy: Under his tutelage, you begin to write and publish. His exertion on your behalf renews his sense of purpose. You become a team, Fitzgerald and Perkins all over again. Soon he's promoting a new generation of talent—your disciples—and you're evolving from your Early to your Later Period.

"The old crew would have thought of that," he says. "Siamese fighting fish in the water cooler."

You try to think of a retort along the lines of "a scale off the fish that bit you," but it doesn't quite come.

"Where are you headed?"

"Lunch," you say, before you can think better of it. The last time you told Alex you were on your way to lunch you needed a stretcher to get you back to the office.

He consults his watch. "Not a bad idea. Mind if I join you?"

By the time you compose an excuse it seems too late, indeed rude, to say that you're meeting a friend. You don't have to match him drink for drink. You don't have to drink anything, although one wouldn't kill you. One pop would cut neatly through this headache. You'll just tell him you've got a big piece going to press. He'll understand. You could use a friendly presence. You might even confide in him. Tell him some of your problems. Alex is a man familiar with trouble.

"Have you ever considered getting an MBA?" he asks. He has taken you to a steakhouse off Seventh Avenue, a smoky place favored by *Times* reporters and other heavy drinkers. He is dropping ashes on his steak, which lies cold and untouched. Already he has informed you that it is impossible to get a good steak anymore. Beef isn't what it used to be; they force-feed the cattle and inject them with hormones. He is on his third vodka martini. You are trying to stretch your second.

"I'm not saying necessarily go into business. But write about it. That's the subject now. The guys who understand business are going to write the new literature. Wally Stevens said money is a kind of poetry, but he didn't follow his own advice." He tells you there was the golden age of Papa and Fitzgerald and Faulkner, then a silver age in which he played a modest role. He thinks we're now in a bronze age, and that fiction has nowhere to go. It can run but it can't hide.

The new writing will be about technology, the global economy, the electronic ebb and flow of wealth. "You're a smart boy," he says. "Don't be seduced by all that crap about garrets and art."

He flags down two more martinis, even though your second has yet to run dry.

"I envy you," he says. "What are you—twenty-one?"

"Twenty-four."

"Twenty-four. Your whole life ahead of you. You're single, right?"

First you say no, and then yes. "Yes. Single."

"You've got it made," he says, although he has just informed you that the world you are going to inherit will have neither good beef nor good writing. "My liver's shot," he adds. "My liver's gone to hell and I've got emphysema."

The waiter comes with the drinks and asks about Alex's steak, if there is anything wrong, if he would prefer something else. Alex says there's nothing particularly wrong with it and tells him to take it away.

"You know why there's so much homosexuality now?" he says after the waiter is gone.

You shake your head.

"It's because of all the goddamned hormones

they inject into the beef. An entire generation's grown up on it." He nods and looks you straight in the eye. You assume a thoughtful, manly expression. "So, who are you reading these days," he asks. "Tell me who the young hotshots are, the up-and-comers."

You mention a couple of your recent enthusiasms, but presently his attention drifts away and his eyelids flutter. You revive him by asking about Faulkner, with whom he shared an office in Hollywood for a couple of months in the forties. He tells you about a high-speed three-day carouse soaked with bourbon and studded with bons mots.

Alex hardly notices when you say goodbye to him on the sidewalk. His nose is pointed in the direction of the office, his eyes glazed with alcohol and memories. You are a little glazed yourself and a walk is absolutely necessary by way of clearing the head. It's early. There is still time. You are standing at the corner of Walk and Don't Walk—staring at Mary O'Brien McCann, the Missing Person poster girl—when somebody taps you on the shoulder.

"Hey, man, wanna buy a ferret?"

The guy is about your age, acne scars, skittish eyes. He is holding a leash attached to an animal that looks not unlike a dachshund in a fur coat.

"That's a ferret?"

"Guaranteed."

"What does he do?"

"Makes a great conversation piece. You'll meet a lot of chicks, I'm telling you. You got any rats in your apartment, he'll take care of that. His name's Fred."

Fred is an elegant-looking animal, apparently well behaved, though you have been known to be deceived by first appearances—witness the Austin Healey you bought with a junkyard under the hood and the genuine Cartier watch. Or the time you picked out a wife. It occurs to you that this would be the perfect mascot for the Department—a real live ferret for the fact finders. You don't really need a pet, you can't even take care of yourself, but perhaps Fred would be the ideal companion for Clara. A parting gift; a token of your affection.

"How much?"

"A hundred."

"Fifty."

"All right, eighty-five. My lowest."

You tell him you'll have to shop around. He gives you a business card with the name of an adult magazine shop. "Ask for Jimmy," he says.

"I got boas and monkeys, too. My prices can't be beat. *I'm* insane."

You walk across town, east on Forty-seventh, past the windows of the discount jewelry stores. A hawker with an armful of leaflets drones in front of a shop door: "Gold and silver, buy and sell, gold and silver, buy and sell." No questions asked on the buying end, you presume. Chain-snatchers welcome. You stop to admire an emerald tiara, the perfect gift for your next queen for a day. Fantasy shopping. Of course, when you have money you will not stop here. You're not going to wow your dream girl with a jewelry box that reads Gem-O-Rama. You'll head straight for Tiffany or Cartier. Sit in a chair in the president's office and have them fetch the merchandise for your inspection.

Hasidim hurry up and down the street, holding their hats, stopping to confer with one another, taking care not to eyeball the women in miniskirts. You examine the wares in the window of the Gotham Book Mart, and take note of the sign: WISE MEN FISH HERE.

At Fifth Avenue you cross and walk up to Saks. You stop in front of a window. Inside the window is a mannequin which is a replica of Amanda—your wife, the model. To form the cast for the mannequin, Amanda lay face down in a vat of latex batter for ninety minutes, breathing through a straw. You haven't seen her in the flesh since she left for the last trip to Paris, a few days after she did the cast. You stand in front of the window and try to remember if this was how she really looked.

**LES
JEUX
SONT
FAITS**

You met her in Kansas City, where
you had gone to work as a reporter after college.
You had lived on both coasts and abroad; the
heartland was until then a large blank. You felt
that some kind of truth and American virtue lurked
thereabouts, and as a writer you wanted to tap
into it.

Amanda grew up smack in the heart of the
heartland. You met her in a bar and couldn't
believe your luck. You never would have worked
up the hair to hit on her, but she came right up

and started talking to you. As you talked you thought: *She looks like a goddamned model and she doesn't even know it*. You thought of this ingenuousness as being typical of the heartland. You pictured her backlit by a sunset, knee-deep in amber waves of grain. Her lanky, awkward grace put you in mind of a newborn foal. Her hair was the color of wheat, or so you imagined; after two months in Kansas you had yet to see any wheat. You spent most of your time at zoning-board meetings duly reporting on variances for shopping malls and perc tests for new housing developments. At night, because your apartment was too quiet, you went to bars with a book.

She seemed to think you came from Manhattan. Everyone in Kansas thought you came from New York City, whether you said Massachusetts, New England, or just East Coast. She asked about Fifth Avenue, The Carlyle, Studio 54. Obviously, from her magazine reading she knew more about these places than you did. She had visions of the Northeast as a country club rolling out from the glass and steel towers of Manhattan. She asked about the Ivy League, as if it were some kind of formal organization, and later that night she introduced you to her roommate as a member of it.

Within a week she moved in with you. She was working for a florist, and thought she might eventually like to attend classes at the university. Your education daunted and excited her. Her desire to educate herself was touching. She asked you for reading lists. She talked about the day your book would be published. All your plans were aimed at Gotham. She wanted to live on Central Park and you wished to join the literary life of the city. She sent away for the catalogues of universities in New York and typed the résumés which you sent out.

The more you learned of Amanda's early life, the less surprised you were at her desire to start afresh. Her father left home when she was six. He did something on oil rigs, and the last Amanda heard he was in Libya. She got a Christmas card with a picture of a mosque. When she was ten she moved with her mother to a cousin's farm in Nebraska. It was not much of a home. Her mother married a feed-and-grain salesman, and they moved to K.C. The salesman wasn't home often and, when he was, he was either abusive or amorous to both mother and daughter. Amanda had to look after herself; you gathered her mother didn't much care about her. She left home when she was sixteen and moved in with a boyfriend, who lasted until a few months before she met you. He left a note explaining that he was moving to California.

Hers was a childhood grimmer than most, and whenever you were inclined to find her lacking, you reminded yourself to give her credit for endurance.

In the eight months you lived together in Kansas City you visited her mother only once. Amanda was skittish and snappy on the way out. You pulled up to a trailer home on a treeless street. She introduced her mother as Dolly. The feed-and-grain salesman, you surmised, was no longer in the picture. There was tremendous tension in the cramped living room. Dolly chain-smoked Kools, flirted with you, and tossed offhand jabs at Amanda. You could see that Dolly was used to trading on her looks and that she loathed and envied her daughter's youth. The resemblance between the two was strong, except that Dolly had a bust—a difference she alluded to several times. You could tell Amanda was ashamed of her, ashamed of the velvet painting on the wall and the unwashed dishes in the sink, ashamed that her mother was a beautician. When Dolly went to the bathroom—"to freshen up," as she put it—Amanda picked up the souvenir Statue of Liberty on top of the television set and said,

"Look at this. It's my mother all over." She seemed afraid that you would think it was her possession, her taste, afraid that you would identify her with Dolly.

Two years later Dolly was invited to the wedding back East. Amanda was relieved when she couldn't make it. Her father's invitation was Returned to Sender bearing a collection of Arabic postmarks, Address Unknown. There was no bride's side at the church, no one except a distant, aged aunt and uncle to indicate that Amanda's past extended farther back than the day she arrived with you in New York. That seemed to be just how she wanted it.

If your parents were not thrilled with the living-together arrangement, they went out of their way to give her a home when you returned to the East Coast. Your mother never turned away a stray dog, or heard about the plight of children in other parts of the world without volunteering her time or reaching for her checkbook, and she greeted Amanda as if she were a refugee. Amanda's need to belong was part of her attraction. It was as if you came across one of those magazine ads—"You could turn the page, or you could save a child's life"—and the child in question was *right there*, charming and eager to please. Long before the wedding she took to calling your parents "Mom

and Dad," and the house in Bucks County "home."
You were all suckered. Your father once asked
you if you didn't think the vast difference in your
backgrounds might be a problem in the long haul,
the only expressed reservation you remember.

Before you had given the subject much thought,
there was on all sides the imminent assumption
of marriage. After two years of living together,
it seemed the thing to do. You were uneasy—
had you lived enough of your life yet?—but your
scrutiny of the situation yielded no decisive ob-
jections. Amanda was desperate for it. She was
always saying she knew you would leave her
someday, as if you had to behave like all the other
swine in her life, and apparently she thought that
marriage would delay or perhaps even cancel your
flight. You did not feel that you could open quite
all of your depths to her, or fathom hers, and
sometimes you feared she didn't have any depths.
But you finally attributed this to an unrealistic,
youthful idealism. Growing up meant admitting
you couldn't have everything.

The proposal was not entirely romantic. It came
about after you had stayed out late with some
friends at a party Amanda did not choose to attend. You crept in toward dawn and found her
awake watching TV in the living room. She was
furious. She said you acted like a single man. She

wanted someone who would make a commit-
ment. She didn't want the kind of bum her mother
kept bringing home. Your guilt was aggravated
by a headache. The sun was coming up and you
felt that she was right. You were a bad boy. You
wanted to amend your life. You wanted to make
it up to Amanda for the shitty life she had had
as a kid. You told her you would marry her, and,
after sulking *de rigueur,* she accepted.

You arrived in New York with the question of
what Amanda was going to do. She had talked
about college, but lost interest when it came time
to fill out the applications. She wasn't sure what
she wanted to do. For several months she watched
TV.

People were always telling Amanda she could
be a model. One day she stopped in at one of
the agencies and came home with a contract.

At the start she hated modeling and you took
this as a sign of character. It was okay by you as
long as she didn't take it seriously. When she
started bringing home all this money it seemed
even more okay. Once a week she said she was
going to quit. She hated the photographers, the
hustlers and the hype. She hated the *models.* She

felt guilty making all this money on her looks, in which she didn't believe anyway. You asked her if she thought being a secretary was fun. You told her to stick with it long enough to salt away some money, and then she could do whatever she wanted.

You thought it was kind of kinky that she was doing this as long as she was slumming, as long as she wasn't really a model. You both joked about the *real* models, the ones who developed ulcers over pimples and thought menopause set in at twenty-five. You both despised people who thought an invitation to X's birthday bash at Magique was an accomplishment equal to swimming the English Channel. But you went to X's birthday bash anyway, with your tongues in your cheeks, and while Amanda circulated you snorted some of X's very good friend's private stash of pink Peruvian flake in the upstairs lounge.

Her agent used to lecture her, telling her that as a professional she had to take it more seriously, stop getting ten-dollar haircuts and start going to the right places. Amanda was amused. She did a fine imitation of this agent, a modeling star of the fifties who had the manner of a dorm mother and the heart of a pimp. Over the months, though, you started eating at better restaurants and

Amanda started getting her hair cut on the Upper East Side.

The first time she went to Italy for the fall showings, she cried at the airport. She reminded you that in a year and a half you had never spent a night apart. She said to hell with it, she would skip Italy, screw modeling. You convinced her to go. She called every night from Milan. Later on these separations did not seem so traumatic. You postponed your honeymoon indefinitely because she had to do the spring collections three days after the wedding.

You were busy with your own work. There were nights you got home after she was asleep. You looked at her across the breakfast nook in the morning and it often seemed that she was looking through the walls of the apartment building halfway across the continent to the plains, as if she had forgotten something there and couldn't quite remember what it was. Her eyes reflected the flat vastness of her native ground. She sat with her elbows on the butcher-block table, twisting a strand of hair in her fingers, head cocked to one side as if she were listening for voices on the wind. There was always something elusive about her, a quality you found mysterious and unsettling. You suspected she herself couldn't quite identify the longing that she variously attached to you, to her job, to having and spending, to her missing father, and that she had once attached to the idea of getting married. You *were* married. And still she was looking for something. But then she would cook you a special dinner, leave love notes in your briefcase and your bureau drawers.

A few months ago she was packing for a trip to Paris when she began to cry. You asked her what was wrong. She said she was nervous about the trip. By the time the cab arrived she was fine. You kissed at the door. She told you to water the plants.

The day before she was due home, she called. Her voice sounded peculiar. She said she wasn't coming home. You didn't understand.

"You got a later flight?"

"I'm staying," she said.

"For how long?"

"I'm sorry. I wish you well. Really I do."

"What are you saying?"

"I'm going to Rome for *Vogue* next week and then Greece for location work. My career is really taking off over here. I'm sorry. I don't mean to hurt you."

"Career?" you said. "Since when is modeling a fucking *career*?"

"I'm sorry," she said. "I have to go now."

You demanded an explanation. She said she had been unhappy. Now she was happy. She needed space. She said goodbye and promptly hung up.

After three days of transatlantic telexes and calls you located her in a hotel on the Left Bank. She sounded weary when she picked up the phone.

"Is there another man," you asked. This was the track your mind had followed for three sleepless nights. That wasn't the point, she said, but yes, there was. He was a photographer. Probably the sort who called himself an *artist*. You couldn't believe it. You reminded her that she had said that they were all fags.

She said, "*Au contraire*, Pierre," ripping the last strained tissues that held your heart intact. When you called again later she had checked out.

A few days afterward, a man purporting to be her lawyer called. The easiest thing all around, he said, would be for you to sue his client for sexual abandonment. Just a legal term, he said. His client, your wife, would not contest anything. You could split the possessions fifty-fifty, although she drew the line at the sterling and crystal. You hung up and wept. *Sexual Abandonment*. He called again a few days later to announce that the car and the joint checking account were yours. You said you wanted to know where Amanda was. He called back and asked how much money you would settle for. You called him a pimp. "I want an explanation," you said.

This was months ago. You haven't told anyone at work. When they ask about Amanda you say she's fine. Your father doesn't know. When you talk to him on the phone you tell him everything is swell. You believe your filial duty is to appear happy and prosperous. It is the least you can do for him after all he's done for you. You don't want him to feel bad, and as it is, he has plenty to worry about. Then, too, you feel that spilling the beans would be irrevocable. He would never be able to forgive Amanda. As long as there is a chance she might still return, you don't want him to know about her treachery. You want to tough it out on your own. You plead work, commitments, parties with Nobel Prize–winners as your reasons for staying in the city, even though home is only two hours away. Sooner or later you will have to go, but you want to put it off as long as possible.

◻

You stand in front of Saks Fifth Avenue and stare at the mannequin. Sometime last week, when you started shouting at it, a policeman came over and told you to move along. This is just how she looked at the end, the blank stare, the lips tight and reticent.

When did she become a mannequin?

◨

Back at the office, your resolution to pursue the facts of the recent French elections has staled. A little nap in one of the upstairs offices would be the thing. But you've got to hang in there. You make yourself a cup of instant espresso with four tablespoons of Maxim. Megan tells you there have been three calls for you: one from the president of the Polar Explorers, one from France and another from your brother Michael.

You go into Clara's office to snag the page proofs but they're not on the desk. You ask Rittenhouse about this, and he tells you that Clara called and asked to have the proofs delivered to Typesetting. She also told him to messenger a photocopy down to her apartment.

"Well," you say, not sure whether you are horrified or relieved. "That's that, I guess."

"Do you have any last-minute changes," Rittenhouse asks. "I'm sure there's time for some last-minute changes."

You shake your head. "I'd have to go back about three years to make all the necessary changes."

"I don't suppose you remembered that bagel," Megan says. "Not to worry. I'm not really hungry anyway. I shouldn't be eating lunch."

You apologize. You beg her pardon. You tell her there are so damn many things on your mind. You have a bad memory for details. You can tell her the date of the Spanish Armada, but you couldn't even guess at the balance of your checkbook. Every day you misplace your keys or your wallet. That's one of the reasons you're always late. It's so hard just getting in here every morning, let alone remembering all that you're supposed to do. You can't pay attention when people talk to you. So many little things. The big things— at least the big things declare open combat. But these details . . . When you are engaged, life or death, with the main army—then to have these niggardly details sniping at you from the goddamned trees . . .

"I'm so sorry, Meg. I'm really, really sorry. I'm just fucking everything up."

Everyone is looking at you. Megan comes over and puts her arm around your shoulders. She strokes your hair.

"Take it easy," she says. "It's only a bagel. Sit

down, just sit down and relax. Everything's going to be all right."

Somebody brings you a glass of water. Along the windows, the potted plants form a jungle skyline, a green tableau of the simple life. You think of islands, palm trees, food-gathering. Escape.

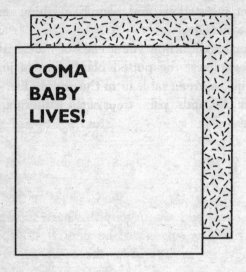

COMA BABY LIVES!

Everyone is so kind. They all want to cover for you, take care of the work on your desk. You have been inclined of late to underestimate the goodness of the race. But Megan, Wade, Rittenhouse—they want you to relax, go home. You don't want to go home. Your apartment is a chamber of horrors. There are instruments of torture in the kitchen cabinets, rings in the walls, spikes on the bed. That place is must-to-avoid. Now that you have released your cramped grip on your responsibilities here, the office seems a quaint place, a place you love because you've already lost your lease.

You wander down to the library to browse through back issues. Marianne, the archivist, is glad to see you. She doesn't get many visitors. All day long she slices issues of the magazine into column-width strips and pastes them into file volumes by author, subject and year. She can tell you where everything is. At first she is disappointed that you are not looking for anything in particular, then amazed when you try to talk to her. Suspicious when you ask where she lives, she gradually warms to the neutral subject of movies. She is a fiend for the comedies of the thirties and forties—Lubitsch, Capra, Cukor. "Have you seen *Trouble in Paradise*," she asks. Oh yes. You certainly have. "Movies aren't what they used to be," she says, then hints that a certain so-called film critic known to both of you has trashy taste, not to mention a filthy mouth. Marianne is loyal to the magazine but concerned about infiltrators and climbers who are trying to subvert it from within. The Druid, she worries, is getting bad advice from flatterers. Ducking into the cage of bound volumes, she comes out with 1976. She flips through the pages and puts her finger under a passage containing a four-letter word, its first appearance in the magazine. Granted, it was only fiction, granted that the author had won the National Book Award. But still . . . The dam is crumbling. She considers it an institutional imperative to maintain standards. "If we don't say No, who will?" You find it touching, almost heartbreaking, this ethic of appearances.

"It's not just that—it's the ads," you say. "Look at the ads. Women doing suggestive things with cigarettes, diamonds set in cleavage, nipples everywhere you look."

"It's everywhere," she agrees. "Do you know what a little boy—not eight or ten years old—said to me on the subway this morning?"

"What was that?"

"I can't even repeat it. It was unbelievable."

You know all about unbelievable; you don't even think about it, much less repeat it.

Later you go up to the empty thirtieth-floor office of a writer on a detox sabbatical. You need a private phone. You practice your spiel aloud, trying out a British accent. You take a deep breath and dial Amanda's agency. You don't recognize the voice on the other end. You identify yourself as a photographer and say that you are interested in working with Amanda White. Is she in New

York, by any chance? The woman on the other end is clearly new, else she would not be so forthcoming with the information. Agency policy is to treat all male callers as potential rapists until proven legitimate. This voice tells you that, as a matter of fact, you are in luck, since Amanda has recently returned to New York for a couple of weeks. "She's based in Paris, you know." You ask if she's doing any shows; you'd like to see her on the runway before you book her. The woman mentions a show on Thursday before you hear someone in the background.

"Could I have your name, please?" the woman says, suddenly all vigilance and officiousness. You're already putting the receiver back in its cradle. Now you need only the location of the show, which a quick call to a friend at *Vogue* will provide. In your mind images of revenge and carnage do battle with scenes of tender reconciliation.

Coming back down the inside stairs, you catch a glimpse of Clara marching into the Department. You bolt up the stairs and duck into the Fiction Department Men's Room. You know you will have to face her sooner or later, so it might as well be later. Much later. Your equilibrium is fragile. Perhaps you will meet over drinks someday and laugh about this whole thing. This antic chapter of your life, "Youthful Folly," will follow "Early Promise." The magazine, ever forgiving, will be proud to claim you as one of its own. You'd gladly sleep through the intervening years and wake up when this part is over. In the meantime, a truckload of Librium and a nice long coma.

You are studying your face in the mirror when the door is opened by Walter Tyler, the travel editor. It's hard to know how to greet Tyler, whether he will stand on the dignity of his position and New England lineage or be just another guy who likes the Yankees. Either way, he'll be offended if you guess wrong. Sometimes the sound of his Christian name in an underling's mouth is sacrilege to his ears. At other times his sense of hale fellowship is offended by a formal address. So this time you nod and say hello.

"I've always wanted to ask someone from Fact," he says as he takes up his position in front of the urinal, "does Clara piss in the Men's Room or the Ladies'?"

Now you've got the cue. "I don't believe she pisses."

"Marvelous," he says. It's taking him a while to get going at the urinal. To fill in the silence he asks "So how do you like it down there?" as if you had joined the staff last week.

"All in all, I'd rather be in Fiction."

He nods and tends to business for a while, then says, "You write, don't you?"

"That seems to be a matter of opinion."

"Hmmmm." He shakes and zips. At the door he turns and fixes you with a serious look. "Read Hazlitt," he says. "That's my advice. Read Hazlitt and write before breakfast every day."

Advice to last a lifetime. Your advice to Walter Tyler is to give it an extra shake or two if he wants to return to his office with dry chinos.

You make for the elevator. Some troll you have never seen sticks his head out of an office door and immediately retracts it. Rounding the corner, you narrowly miss running down the Ghost.

The Ghost cocks his head to one side, peering, his eyelids fluttering. You say good afternoon and identify yourself.

"Yes," he says, as if he knew all along who it was. He likes to give the impression that his reclusiveness is an advantage, that he knows more than you could ever expect to. You've only seen him once before, this legend, this man who has been working on a single article for seven years.

You excuse yourself and slide past. For his part, the Ghost glides away silently, as if on wheels. You escape the building without incident. Your jacket, small ransom, is back in the Department.

It is a warm, humid afternoon. Spring, apparently. Late April or early May. Amanda left in January. There was snow on the ground the morning she called, a whiteness that turned gray and filthy by noon and then disappeared down the sewer grates. Later that morning the florist called about the bouquet you ordered for her return. Everything becomes symbol and irony when you have been betrayed.

You slip into a bar on Forty-fourth, a nice anonymous Irish place where no one has anything on his mind except drinking and sports. On a big video screen at the far end of the long wooden bar is some kind of sporting event. You take a stool and order a beer, then turn your attention to the screen. Basketball. You didn't realize basketball was in season this time of year, but you like the soothing back-and-forth movement of the ball. The guy sitting next to you swivels and says, "Those fucking bums don't know how to handle the full court press."

You nod and fill your mouth with beer. He seems to expect a response, so you ask him what period it is.

He looks you up and down, as if you were carrying a volume of poetry or wearing funny shoes. "Third *quarter*," he answers. Then he turns away.

You keep meaning to cultivate an expertise in

spectator sport. More and more you realize that sports trivia is crucial to male camaraderie. You keenly feel your ignorance. You are locked out of the largest fraternity in the country. You'd like to be the kind of guy who can walk into a bar or an eatery and break the ice with a Runyonism about the stupidity of a certain mid-season trade. Have something to hash out with truck drivers and stockbrokers alike. In high school, you went in for lone-wolf sports—tennis and skiing. You're not really sure what a zone defense is. You don't understand the sports metaphors in the political columns. Men don't trust a man who missed the Super Bowl. You would like to devote a year to watching every athletic event on ABC and reading all fifty-two issues of *Sports Illustrated*. In the meantime your strategy is to view one playoff game in each sport so as to manage remarks like, "How about that slap shot by Lafleur in the third period against Boston?" Third quarter?

It's five-twenty and raining when you leave the bar. You walk down to the Times Square subway station. You pass signs for GIRLS, GIRLS, GIRLS, and one that says YOUNG BOYS. Then, in a stationery store, DON'T FORGET MOTHER'S DAY. The rain starts coming down harder. You wonder if you own an umbrella. You've left so many in taxis. Usually, by the time the first raindrop hits the street, there are men on every corner selling umbrellas. Where do they come from, you have often wondered, and where do they go when it's not raining? You imagine these umbrella peddlers huddled around powerful radios waiting for the very latest from the National Weather Service, or maybe sleeping in dingy hotel rooms with their arms hanging out the windows, ready to wake at the first touch of precipitation. Maybe they have a deal with the taxi companies, you think, to pick up all the left-behind umbrellas for next to nothing. The city's economy is made up of strange, subterranean circuits that are as mysterious to you as the grids of wire and pipe under the streets. At the moment, though, you see no umbrella vendors whatsoever.

You wait fifteen minutes on the downtown platform. Everywhere you look you see the Missing Person. An announcement is made that the express is out of service. The tunnel smells of wet clothing and urine. The voice comes over the speaker again to say that the local will be delayed twenty minutes because of a fire on the tracks. You push through the crowd and ascend to the street.

It is still raining. Getting a cab is a long shot. Knots of people on every corner wave their arms at the passing traffic. You walk down Seventh to the bus stop, where some twenty souls huddle in the shelter. A bus packed with grim faces goes by and doesn't stop.

An old woman breaks from the shelter and chases her ride. "Stop! You stop here!" She whacks the rear of the bus with her umbrella.

Another bus pulls over and disgorges passengers. The sheltered mob clutch umbrellas, purses and briefcases, prepared to fight for seats; but once the bus unloads it's nearly empty. The driver, a massive black man with sweat rings under his arms, says "Take it easy," and his voice commands respect.

You sit down up front. The bus lurches into traffic. Below Fortieth Street the signs on the corners change from Seventh Avenue to Fashion Avenue as you enter the garment district. Amanda's old stomping grounds. Above Forty-second they sell women without clothes and below they sell clothes with women.

At the Thirty-fourth Street stop there is a commotion at the door. "Zact change," the bus driver says. A young man standing by the change box is trying to work his hand into the pockets of his skin-tight Calvin Kleins. Peach Lacoste shirt, a mustache that looks like a set of plucked eyebrows. Under one arm he clutches a small portfolio and a bulky Japanese paper umbrella. He rests the umbrella against the change box. "Step aside," the bus driver says. "People getting wet out there."

"I know all *about* wet, big guy."

"I just bet you do, Queenie."

Finally he gets his change together and deposits the coins one at a time, with flourishes, and then cocks his hip at the bus driver.

"Move to the rear, Queenie," the bus driver says. "I know you know how to do that."

The young man walks down the aisle with burlesque movements of the hips and wrist. The bus driver turns and watches him go. When he gets all the way back, the driver picks up the Japanese umbrella he left behind. The driver waits until it is quiet and then says, "Hey, Tinker Bell. You forgot your wand."

Everyone watching titters and guffaws. The bus hasn't moved.

Tinker Bell poses at the back of the bus, narrowing his eyes and scowling. Then he smiles. He walks back up the aisle, putting everything he's got into it. He reaches the front and picks up the umbrella. He raises it over his head and brings it down gently on the driver's shoulder, as if he were bestowing knighthood. He does this three times, saying, in a cheery falsetto voice, "Turn to shit, turn to shit, turn to shit."

❏

At your apartment building you discover that you have no keys. They're in the pocket of your jacket, which is back in the Department of Factual Verification. Much as you dislike your apartment, it has a bed in it. You want to sleep. You have attained that fine pitch of exhaustion which might make it possible. You've been thinking about that packet of instant cocoa in the kitchen, *Family Feud* on the TV. You were even thinking you might take some Dickens to bed with you. Run your mind over someone else's pathetic misadventures for a change.

An image of yourself curled up on the sidewalk next to a heat vent with the other bums yields to the slightly less grim prospect of asking the super for the spare set of keys. The super, a huge Greek, has glared at you ever since you forgot to pay the customary tribute of cash or booze for Christmas. His wife is no less formidable, being the one who wears the mustache in the family.

Fortunately, the man who answers the door is one of the cousins, a young man whose lack of English and dubious visa status make him eager to oblige. You mime the problem and within minutes you are at your door with the spare set. An envelope with the logo of Allagash's employer, an ad agency, is taped to the door. Inside, a note:

Coach:

Having this messengered to your digs after numerous calls to reputed place of employ. Don't you keep office hours anymore? It's tiresome, God knows, but one should try to keep up appearances and also be accessible in case of emergencies like present one. To be brief:

A long-anticipated tryst with the libidinous Inge—pin-up Queen manquée—is endangered by visit of cousin from Boston branch of family. I know what you're thinking: A Boston branch of the Allagash clan? But every family has its dark secrets. Said cousin is doing academic gig at NYU and laying over at the Allagash pad. Must be entertained in grand manner. A well-bred young woman, something of an intellect, who would not be charmed by some junior account exec with toothpaste market surveys on the brain. This assignment calls for nothing less than a speaker of French, a reader of *The New York Review of Books* and that inexpressible guileless charm with which your name is synonymous. Don't let me down,

Coach, and everything I possess, including a portion of Bolivia's finest, not to mention my undying gratitude and fealty, is yours. Have taken liberty of informing cousin, one Vicky Hollins, that you will be meeting her at the Lion's Head at seven-thirty, to be joined by self and Inge at earliest possible convenience. Described you as cross between young F. Scott Fitz-Hemingway and the later Wittgenstein, so dress accordingly.

YRS. IN CHRIST, T.A.

P.S. Should you get lucky with cousin or inflict rare social disease this office will deny all knowledge of your actions.

The presumption of Allagash appalls you. When you call his office to decline the invitation, he has already left. Well, it's his cousin and his problem. The thought of the Allagash genes and the Boston climate is a frightening one. His brief description suggests a prig, a wearer of plaid tartan skirts, a former contender on the green New England hockey fields and a noncontender in the Looks Department. Born into the manner that Clara has been faking ever since she went to Vassar. You will unplug the phone and say you never got the letter.

You switch on the tube and throw yourself on the couch. Much fun on *Family Feud*. Ten grand rides on a question about garden tools; Richard Dawson flexes his eyebrows. But you keep glancing at the clock. By seven-twenty you are on your feet, pacing between the two rooms, kicking your laundry into the corners. If you know Tad, he won't even make it to the Lion's Head and the poor girl will be left to the slender mercies of all those aspiring actors and failed writers. A few friendly drinks with her wouldn't kill you. You throw on a jacket and head out.

You arrive ten minutes late. It's two deep along the bar and no sign of Allagash. No sign of anybody wearing a plaid tartan skirt and Allagash features.

In the middle of your beer you spot a woman standing alone beside the coatrack, holding a drink and reading a paperback. She looks up from time to time and then returns to her reading. You watch her eyes as they move around the room. Her face is intelligent. The hair is somewhere between strawberry and gold, you can't tell in this light. That she could be the Boston Allagash is too much to hope. Boots, jeans and a black silk shirt. Not a patch of madras or tartan on her.

The hell with Allagash and his race. You would like to speak to this woman, ask her if she's eaten dinner. Perhaps she is the one who could make you forget your cares and woes, start eating breakfast, take up jogging. You edge in closer. The book in her hand is Spinoza's *Ethics*. No flies on that. She looks up again and you catch her eye.

"We don't get many Rationalists in here," you say.

"I'm not surprised," she says. "Too dark." Her voice is like gravel spread with honey. She holds a smile just long enough to encourage you and then returns to her book. You wish you could remember something about Spinoza, besides the fact that he was excommunicated.

Allagash appears in the door. You consider hiding out in the Men's Room, but he spots you and comes over. Tad shakes your hand. Then he plants a kiss on the philosopher's cheek.

Introductions, brief confusion about whether everyone has met. Allagash tells you, with a deprecating roll of his eyes, that Vicky is studying philosophy at Princeton. He introduces you as a literary cult celebrity whose name has not yet reached the provinces.

"Hate to dash out again. But I said seven-thirty and Inge thought I said ten. So she's still in *media* dress, as we say. Got to get crosstown and pick her up. But let's by all means meet for dinner."

He consults his watch. "Let's say nine-thirty. Better make it ten. Ten o'clock at Raoul's. Don't forget." He slips a glass vial into your pocket while he's kissing Vicky. Then he's gone in a wake of camel's hair.

Vicky seems confused by her cousin's hospitality. "Did you catch all that?"

"More or less." You know you will not see Tad for the rest of the night.

"He said seven-thirty and his date thought he said ten?"

"It's a common mistake."

"Well," she says, putting her book in her purse. This could have been a very awkward situation, but she's taking it in stride. "What now?"

Allagash has bribed you with a piece of the rock. You could invite her back to your place to share the booty, but somehow you think not. Although you suppose she would appreciate it, you'd like to see if it's possible to get through an evening without chemicals for a change. Hear yourself and another person talk without Speedy Gonzales South American accents.

You ask her if she wants to stay for another drink, and she asks what you want to do. Eventually you ascend the stairs to the street. You think of Plato's pilgrims climbing out of the cave, from the shadow world of appearances toward things as they really are, and you wonder if it is possible to change in this life. Being with a philosopher makes you think.

You linger at the edge of Sheridan Square to watch an acrobat ride a unicycle across a tightrope strung between the fences. A teenager in the crowd turns to Vicky and says, "He did that between the towers of the World Trade Center."

"Can you imagine," a woman asks.

"Sounds like my job," you say.

When the acrobat passes the hat you throw in a buck. You walk west, without any firm destination in mind. Vicky is telling you about her work. She's in her third year of graduate school, came in for an NYU conference at which she will read a rebuttal to an article entitled: "Why There Are No People."

The evening is cool. You find yourself walking the Village, pointing out landmarks and favorite townhouses. Only yesterday you would have considered such a stroll too New Jersey for words, but tonight you remember how much you used to like this part of the city. The whole neighborhood smells of Italian food. The streets have friendly names and cut weird angles into the rectilinear map of the city. The buildings are humble in scale and don't try to intimidate you. Gay giants stride past on hypertrophied thighs, swathed in leather and chains, and they do intimidate you.

Vicky stops in front of an antique shop window on Bleecker and points to a wooden carousel horse, painted red and white, mounted on a pedestal. "I'd like to have the kind of house someday where a carousel horse wouldn't be out of place in the living room."

"How about a jukebox?"

"Oh, definitely. There's always room for a jukebox. And maybe a pinball machine. A really old one with Buck Rogers stuff."

As you resume your walk she describes the house in which she grew up. A rambling Tudor affair on the shore in Marblehead, which started out early in the century as a summer house and, despite the formal dining room, never quite lost its wet-towel ambience. There were empty rooms to play in, and a closed alcove under the stairs which no one could enter without her permission. Pets galore. A gazebo where the four girls had tealess tea parties presided over by Vicky's eldest sister. Their father kept chickens in the boathouse and spent years trying to bring a vegetable patch to life. Every morning he woke up at five and went for a swim. Mother stayed in bed till her daughters and the pets gathered in her room.

What she tells you is enhanced by the increasing animation of her gestures and facial expressions and becomes a vivid image of this childhood Arcadia. You notice for the first time that she has freckles. You didn't know they still made them. You imagine her as a child carrying a bucket of sand down to the beach. You see yourself watching from the bluff, through a time warp, saying: *Someday I will meet this girl.* You want to watch over her through the interval, protect her from the cruelty of schoolchildren and the careless lust of young men. The irrevocable past tense of the narration suggests to you some intervening tragedy. You suspect a snake in the vegetable garden.

"Your parents?" you say.

"Divorced three years ago. Yours?"

"Happy marriage," you say.

"You're lucky."

Lucky is not the word you would have chosen, except maybe out of a hat.

"Do you have any brothers or sisters," she asks.

"Three brothers. The youngest are twins."

"That's nice. Symmetrical, I mean. I've got three sisters. Boys were very mysterious to us."

"I know what you mean."

"Listen. Do we have to meet Tad later?"

"Tad has no intention of meeting us. Or, rather, he has good intentions, but he won't be there."

"Did he tell you that?"

125

"No, it's just that I know him. Tad is always on his way, but he seldom arrives."

"What did he tell you about me," she asks, after you have been seated in the courtyard of a café on Charles Street. She has a conspiratorial smile. She seems to think that your allegiance to Tad will crumble before this new intimacy.

"Not much," you say.

"Come on."

"He tried to build you up. I was expecting a field hockey player with monogrammed knee socks and thick glasses."

She does not press for the compliment. Just smiles and looks down at the menu.

You tell her what a good guy Tad is. You like his energy and his style—*joie de vivre, je ne sais quoi, savoir-faire, sprezzatura*. You are nearly sincere. Having a cousin like Vicky tips the scales in his favor. You are inclined to cut him some slack. Not necessarily the man for a heart-to-heart, but indispensable in a party situation. You tell her that Tad has been a good friend in time of need. If not exactly sensitive, then generous in his own careless way. "Are you two very close," you ask.

"I think he's an ass," she says.

"Exactly." Everything she says is right. She's got you in the palm of her unclenched hand. You love the way she raises her water glass to her lips, the ease she has with her hands and mouth. You are afraid you are staring too intently into her eyes, even though this intimacy does not appear uninvited.

"What's your job like?" she says. "I guess I should be pretty impressed."

"Please don't be. I don't like it much. I don't think they much like me."

"I know people who would kill for a job like that."

You'd rather she wasn't too impressed with a job you may not have the next time you see her. You wish that no one, including yourself, had ever been impressed. You wince to think of all the self-aggrandizement you have heaped on this subject. You describe for her the tedious procedure of factual verification, the long hours over dictionaries, phone books, encyclopedias, government pamphlets. You tell her how you were reprimanded for suggesting stylistic changes.

"I've only known you a couple of hours," Vicky says, "but it doesn't seem to me like your kind of job."

"I don't think it is."

Standing on the corner of West Fourth Street and Seventh Avenue, you are ostensibly waiting for a cab to take Vicky back to Tad's apartment. Empty cabs keep rolling past and you and Vicky continue to talk. You have talked about work, money, Cape Cod, breakfast cereals and the Mind-Body Problem. You have already written down her address and phone number in Princeton. Walking back from the restaurant she took your arm and you have been holding hers ever since. You feel that passing males—at least the heteros—look on with envy. You consider performing an act of inspired madcappery at her behest: stealing the hat from a policeman, or the handcuffs from one of the gay caballeros of Christopher Street. Maybe climb a lamppost and wave her scarf from the top.

"*Now* I *really* have to go," she says.

"I wish you didn't."

"Me too." She steps forward and kisses you. You return the kiss and prolong it. Time passes. You become aroused. You consider asking her back to your apartment, and think better of it. You want to leave this flawless evening intact.

Already you are thinking of the walk home, the review of details and nuances in bed before you sleep, of the phone call which you have promised to make tomorrow morning. You are thinking that Clara Tillinghast can go to hell because tonight you are happy.

PYGMIES,
FERRETS
AND
DOG
CHOW

Over coffee and eggs you read both
Times and *Post*, including sports pages. Coma
Mom is fading fast. Boston wins on the basketball
court, loses in baseball. The waitress has filled
your cup six times and it's only eight-thirty. At
six-thirty you woke like a man accustomed to the
hour, feeling a clarity compounding the exhila-
ration from your night with Vicky and the dread
of your morning with Clara. You called the former when you woke up. She told you Tad never
made it home and that she slept very well once

she convinced the doorman she was a legitimate visitor. You want to call her again, maybe tell her all about your breakfast.

You're at the office by nine-thirty. Meg's already there. She looks embarrassed when she sees you. You can guess what happened yesterday after Clara returned. By now everybody has the story of your incompetence. You don't bother to ask.

Meg, though, can't bear the suspense. She comes over to your desk and says, "Clara's in a rage. She says the French piece is a mess but it's too late to pull it from the issue. There was a big pow-wow last night to decide what to do." You nod your head. "What happened?" she asks, as if an easy answer had inexplicably eluded her.

Rittenhouse comes in and performs his customary greeting, which falls somewhere between a nod and a full bow. You will miss his bow ties and his Edwardian bookkeeper manner. After hanging his scarf and derby on the coatrack he joins Megan at your desk, looking even more grave and mournful than usual.

"We're talking about the French piece," Megan says.

Rittenhouse nods. "I think the way they changed the schedule was disgraceful. Although they must have had their reasons."

"You didn't have nearly enough time," Megan says. "Everybody knows his research is slipshod."

"We're behind you all the way," Rittenhouse says.

There's not much comfort in this, but you appreciate the thought.

Wade saunters in and stops in front of your desk. He looks at you and clicks his tongue. "What kind of flowers do you want on your grave? I already have the epitaph: *He didn't face facts.*"

Megan says, "Not funny, Yasu."

"Well, Jesus. Even Lear had a clown."

"This could've happened to any of us," Megan says. "We've got to stick together."

You shake your head. "It's my own damn fault. I dug my own grave."

"You didn't have enough time," Megan says. "It was a sloppy article."

"We've all seen errors slip through the net," Rittenhouse adds.

"How bad could it be," Megan asks. "You got most of it done, didn't you?"

"I really don't even know," you say. They're wondering: *Could this happen to me?* and you would like to reassure them, tell them it's just you. They're trying to imagine themselves in your shoes, but it would be a tough thing to do. Last night Vicky was talking about the ineffability of inner experience. She told you to imagine what it was like to be a bat. Even if you knew what sonar was and how it worked, you could never know what it feels like to have it, or what it feels like to be a small, furry creature hanging upside down from the roof of a cave. She said that certain facts are accessible only from one point of view— the point of view of the creature who experiences them. You think she meant that the only shoes we can ever wear are our own. Meg can't imagine what it's like for you to be you, she can only imagine herself being you.

You want to thank them for their concern, yet you could never truly explain how this fiasco came about.

The group disperses. It's coming up on ten o'clock. You don't have anything to do. Your hands move around the desk collecting paper clips and pens, rearranging stacks of paper. The Druid sneaks past the door. His eyes meet yours and then he looks away. You feel a touch of heat in the cheeks. His renowned manners have failed him. That is something, at least. Tell your children you were the only man in history snubbed by the Druid.

On your desk is a short story that you have been wanting to read. You follow the lines of print across the page, and it's like driving on ice with bald tires; no traction. You get up and fix yourself a cup of coffee. The others are hunched over their desks. In the quiet you can hear the scratching of pencil lead on paper and the hum of the refrigerator. You go to the window and look down on Forty-fifth Street. Maybe you can spot Clara on her way in and let her have it with a flower pot. Although the pedestrians are indistinct, you can make out a man sitting on the sidewalk playing a guitar. You open the window and stick your head out, but the traffic noise covers the music. Someone taps your hip. Wade is pointing toward the door, where Clara is standing.

"I would like to see you in my office immediately."

Wade whispers, "If I were you I would've jumped."

From the window to Clara's office is a very short distance. Much too short. You are there. She slams the door from the inside, takes the seat in front of the desk and stares you down. She doesn't ask you to sit, so you do. This is shaping up even worse than you anticipated. Still, you feel a measure of detachment, as if you had suffered everything already and this were just a flashback. You wish that you had paid more attention when a woman you met at Heartbreak told you about Zen meditation. Think of all of this as an illusion. She can't hurt you. Nothing can hurt the samurai who enters combat fully resolved to die. You have already accepted the inevitability of termination, as they say. Still, you'd rather not have to sit through this.

"I would like to know what happened."

A dumb question. Far too general. You draw a good breath. "I screwed up." You might add that the writer of the piece in question really screwed up, that you improved the thing immeasurably, and that the change of scheduling was ill-advised. But you don't.

"You screwed up."

You nod. It's true. In this case, however, honesty doesn't make you feel a whole lot better. You're having trouble meeting her glare.

"May I be so bold as to ask for a little elaboration? Really, I'm interested."

Sarcasm now.

"Just *how* did you screw up, exactly?"

More ways than you can say.

"Well?"

You're already gone. You are out the window with the pigeons. You try to alleviate the terror by thinking how ridiculous her French braids look, like spinnakers on a tugboat. You suspect that deep down she enjoys this. She's been looking forward to it for a long time.

"Do you realize just how serious this is?" she demands. "You have endangered the reputation of this magazine. We have built a reputation for scrupulous accuracy with regard to matters of fact. Our readers depend on us for the truth."

You would like to say, Whoa! Block that jump from facts to truth, but she is off and running.

"Every time this magazine goes to press that reputation is on the line, and when the current issue hits the stands you will have compromised that reputation, perhaps irretrievably. Do you know that in fifty years of publication there has only been one printed retraction?"

Yes, you know.

"Have you considered that everyone on the staff will suffer as a result of your carelessness?"

Clara's office is none too large under the best of circumstances, and it is getting smaller by the minute. You raise your hand. "Can I ask what errors you have found?"

She has the list ready to hand: Two accents reversed, an electoral district in central France incorrectly identified as northern, a minister ascribed to the wrong department. "This is just what I've been able to find so far. I'm scared to death of what I'll uncover as I go along. The proofs are a mess. I can't tell what you've verified and what you haven't. The point is, you have not followed standard procedure, which by this time should be second nature to you, which procedure is thoroughly outlined in your manual, which procedure is the net result of many years of collective labor, and proper application of which ensures that, insofar as possible, errors of fact do not appear in this magazine."

Clara is red in the face. Although Wade claims she has recently taken up jogging, her wind is lousy.

"Do you have anything to say for yourself?"

"I don't think so."

"This isn't the first time. I've given you the benefit of the doubt before. You seem unable to perform the duties required for this job."

You're not about to take issue with anything she says. You would confess to all of the crimes detailed in the *Post* today in exchange for an exit visa. You nod your head gravely.

"I'd like to hear what you have to say."

"I assume I'm fired."

She looks surprised. She drums her fingers on the desk and glowers. You're pleased that her hands are shaking. "That's correct," she says at last. "Effective immediately."

"Anything else?" you say, and when she doesn't answer you stand up to go. Your legs are trembling, but you don't think she notices.

"I'm sorry," she says as you open the door.

In a stall of the Men's Room you wait for composure to return. Despite your relief, and your feeling that you got no worse than you expected, your hands are twitching to the beat of your knees. Pointlessly exploring your pockets, you come up with a small glass vial, Tad's gift. In terms of improving your mood, this might be just what the doctor ordered. Or precisely not; bad medicine.

You shake a healthy snort onto the back of your hand. Lifting hand to face, you lose your grip on the vial, which drops with sickening accuracy into the toilet bowl, bounces once against the porcelain and then submerges with an insolent splash that resembles the sound of a very large brown trout spitting out the hook of a very small and painstakingly presented dry fly.

Maybe this isn't your day. You should've checked your horoscope in the *Post*.

Huddled around Rittenhouse's desk, the others fall silent when you return.

"Well?" Megan says.

Though your knees are still shaking, you have this strange feeling of omnipotence. You could dive out the window and fly over the rooftops. You could pick up your desk with one hand. Your former colleagues carry the stamp of oppression on their brows.

"It's been nice working with you."

"They didn't," Megan says. "They couldn't."

"They did."

"What exactly did she say," Rittenhouse asks.

"The gist of it is that I'm fired."

"They can't do that," Megan says.

"Perhaps we could take your case to the employee arbitration committee," Rittenhouse says. "As you know, I'm a member of the committee."

You shake your head. "Thanks, but I don't think so."

"Well, at least they could allow you to resign if that's what you want to do," Wade says.

"It doesn't matter," you say. "It really doesn't."

They want to hear exactly what was said, and you oblige them as well as you can. They advise

139

you to make a stand, appeal the decision, ask for clemency, plead special circumstances. They are not convinced that you'd rather switch than fight. Clara does not reappear. Wade thinks you ought to seize this opportunity for a dramatic parting gesture. He suggests hanging a moon in the Druid's office. When Megan asks what you're going to do now, you say you don't know.

"No point in sticking around here. I'll pick up my things tomorrow."

"Can we have lunch tomorrow," Megan asks. "I'd really like to talk to you."

"Sure. Lunch tomorrow. I'll see you then."

You shake hands all around. Megan catches you at the elevator. "I forgot to tell you. Your brother Michael called again. He sounds really eager to talk to you."

"Thanks. I'll call him. Thanks for everything."

Megan puts her hands on your shoulders and kisses you. "Don't forget lunch."

Down on the street, you clamp your sunglasses to your face and wonder where to go. An old question, it seems to come up more and more frequently. You've lost whatever bravado you possessed a few minutes ago. It's just beginning to sink in that you have lost your job. You are no longer associated with the famous magazine where, in time, you might have become an editor or a staff writer. You remember how excited your father was when you got the job, and know how he's going to feel when he hears you have been fired.

You go over and listen to the sidewalk guitarist. He's playing blues, and every phrase is aimed directly between your third and fourth ribs. You listen to "Ain't Got No Home," "Baby Please Don't Go," "Long Distance Call." You turn away when he starts into "Motherless Children."

On Forty-second near Fifth a kid falls into stride beside you.

"Loose joints. Genuine Hawaiian sens. Downers and uppers."

You shake your head. The kid looks all of thirteen.

"Got coke. Got coke if you wannit. Uncut Peruvian flake. Closest you're gonna get to God these days."

"How much?"

"Fifty dollar the half."

"Half what? Half borax and half mannitol?"

"Pure stuff. Uncut."

"Sure thing. Thirty-five."

"I'm a businessman. Not a fie-lanthropuss."

"I can't do fifty."

"Forty-five. You're robbing me."

You follow the kid into the park behind the library. Look both ways before you enter. His brother may be waiting with a baseball bat. Two elderly male civilians are throwing bread at the pigeons. The kid leads you over to a big tree where he tells you to wait. Then he runs to the other side of the park. You can't believe you're doing this. Encouraging juvenile delinquency. Wasting your money on street toot. The kid comes running out from behind the fountain.

"I want a taste."

"Shit," he says. "Who you think you are—John DeLorean? You be buying a half. I'm telling you it's good."

The classic standoff. His salesman's smile is disappearing. You suddenly realize you are about to be ripped off, but you hang on to the hope of a buzz.

"Let me see it at least." He walks behind the tree and opens the packet. You're buying some kind of white powder and the weight looks about right, not that this means much. You give him the money. He stuffs it in his pocket and backs off, watching you as he retreats.

As long as you are relatively secluded you figure you'll try some. You use your office key for a spoon. The first taste is like Drano. The second time you're ready for it, and it's not so bad. Still, it feels like your nose is emitting sparks. Whatever the stuff is, you hope it's not lethal. You hope there's something South American in the mix. After bumping yourself up again you fold the packet. You *think* you can feel a lift coming on. You want to go somewhere, do something, talk to someone, but it's only eleven-thirty in the morning and everyone else in the world has a job.

◼

Much later, near midnight, you return to the office. Tad Allagash is with you. You are both in high spirits. You have decided that you are better off without that piss-ant job, that it is a good thing you got out when you did. A longer tenure in the Department of Factual Verification would have eventually resulted in an incurable case of anal retentiveness. You're well shut of the place. This conclusion does not absolve Clara Tillinghast of her many crimes against humanity, and particularly against you. Tad casts it as a matter of honor. In his part of the country these matters are settled with horsewhips and ivory-headed canes. He says the caning and horsewhipping of libelous editors has a long, dignified history. The present case, however, calls for something more subtle. The better part of the night has been devoted to devising and executing the proper response. Part of the plan involved getting in touch with Richard Fox, the hatchet man, and telling him some of the nasty secrets to which you have become privy after two years at the magazine. You were inclined to let it slide, but Tad appealed to your fighting spirit. He placed the call and got Fox's answering service. He left a message, calling himself Deep Shoat, an inside source, and promised major revelations. He left Clara's number. You proceeded to phase two.

The nightwatchman nods at your employee ID card and tells you to sign the book. You sign in as Ralph Kramden and Ed Norton. Tad explains that your errand is urgent; First Amendment issues are at stake. The watchman is used to writers coming and going at strange hours, and doesn't have the energy to worry about two more drunks. He points to the freight elevator and then goes back to his wrestling magazine. He doesn't even ask about the suitcase.

When the elevator begins to ascend, shrill, birdlike noises issue from the bag. The sound of the animal's distress gives you pause. This is probably a bad idea. You're not particularly worried about Clara, but you feel sorry for Fred the Ferret in his role of unwitting accomplice.

"*Pas de* sweat," Tad says. "This is almost too easy. Maybe we should have tried for the wolf cub." Initially Tad wanted to get hold of a bat, but when you mentioned the ferret his eyebrows climbed his forehead in delight.

The door opens on the twenty-ninth floor. You both stand inside the elevator, listening. It's quiet. Tad looks at you inquisitively. You nod and step out into the reception area. Tad follows. The whoosh of the elevator doors sounds like a passing freight train. There is a hollow echo of cables and gears, and then it's quiet again. Tad leans over and whispers in your ear, "Take no prisoners."

You lead the way down the hall, carrying the suitcase. Up to the corner all the offices are dark, but you remain anxious. The Druid is known for his insane hours and you briefly picture yourself turning the corner and facing him. You would die of mortification. Still, the challenge of the caper has got your adrenaline going. No thrills without chills. The forty-five-degree mirror at the corner shows no lights on farther up.

Clara's door is locked, but that's no problem. You have a key to the Department office, and a key to her office is hidden behind—what else?—

volume K of the *Encyclopaedia Britannica*. It's the work of a moment.

You let yourselves into Clara's office and close the door. "They entered the lair of the dragon," Tad whispers. You turn on the light. "You call this an office?" he says. "It looks like an uppity maid's room."

Now that you're here, you're not quite sure what to do. The ferret is scratching wildly inside the suitcase.

"Where's the leash," you ask.

"I don't have it."

"I gave it to you."

"We don't need the leash. It'll be a better surprise to have the sucker pop out from a desk drawer."

Tad lays the suitcase on the floor and flips the latches, then stands back. "Let him out," he says. You lift the top. Things happen quickly after that. The animal sinks its teeth into your hand. You jerk your arm away. There's a foot of ferret still attached. The pain is terrific. You shake your arm savagely, flinging the thing toward Tad. Fred tears a swath out of Tad's pants leg before landing on the floor, careening around the room, upsetting boxes and finally holing up in the bookshelf behind a row of bound volumes of *Scientific American*.

Your hand is on fire. It is connected by red-hot wires to your brain, which is throbbing inside your skull. You shake your arm, spattering little red droplets on the walls. Tad's face is white. He leans down and gingerly examines the tear in his pants just below the crotch.

"Good Christ! One more inch . . ."

He is interupted by a thump on the door.

"Oh, Jesus!"

There is another thump and then a hoarse voice: "Open up! I know you're in there."

You recognize the voice—it could be worse—and put a finger to your lips. Taking a pencil and pad from Clara's desk, you clumsily write, with your uninjured left hand, *Is the door locked?*

Tad gives you a search-me look.

There is a steady wheezing outside the door and another knock. The doorknob turns one way and then the other. Allagash is poking your arm and mouthing frantic interrogatives. The latch clicks and the door swings open. Alex Hardy stands in the doorway. He nods his head gravely as if you were the very two people he expected to find in Clara's office at midnight. You are trying to devise a quick story that will wash. Tad is brandishing a yardstick that he found behind the door.

"You gave us a scare, Alex. I couldn't imagine who would be wandering around here at this time

147

of night. I was just looking for my wallet. I was
in here this morning . . ."

"Pygmies," Alex says.

Tad looks at you inquisitively. You shrug.

"I am surrounded by pygmies."

You now see that Alex is stupendously drunk.
You wonder if he recognizes you.

"I knew the giants," he says. "I worked with
the giants. The guys whose words went out into
the world and kicked ass. Okay, girls too. Women,
whatever. I'm talking about ambition. I'm talking
about talent. Not like these precious turds around
here. These goddamned pygmies." Alex thumps
his fist on the wall. The ferret leaps out from
hiding and bolts for the door. It snakes its way
between Alex's legs. Alex tries to get out of the
way. The ferret's claws scrabble on the linoleum.
Alex struggles for equilibrium, grabbing first at
the door frame, then, as he starts to fall, at the
coatrack, and finally at a bookshelf, which goes
down with him. The top hooks of the falling coatrack narrowly miss Tad's face. Alex is sprawled
on the floor in a heap of books. You're not sure
how hard he hit.

"Let's get out before he comes to," Tad says.

"I can't leave him like this." You crouch down
and check him out. He's breathing; already the
office smells like liquor.

"Come on. Do you want to *explain* what we're doing here? Let's go."

You clear some of the books from Alex's chest and stretch his legs out. Down the hall a phone starts ringing.

"He's fine, for Christ's sake. We're dead meat if we get caught in here."

"Get the suitcase," you say. You take the cushion from Clara's chair and put it under Alex's head. His feet are sticking out the door so you can't close it. The elevator takes days to arrive and makes a racket like an All Points Bulletin.

In the lobby, the watchman is still absorbed in his magazine. You keep your hand in your jacket pocket while he unlocks the door to the street. Outside, you both break into a sprint.

Neither of you speaks a word until you're in the cab. At Tad's place you wash and examine the wound while he changes his pants. At first you're concerned. You're trying to remember the last time you had a tetanus shot when suddenly you think of rabies. The signature of the teeth is clearly visible between your thumb and index finger. The punctures are deep but not wide. Tad assures you that stitches aren't necessary. He says that if the animal was rabid, it would not have been so friendly before you put it in the suitcase. He pours a glass of vodka over the wound. You're eager to be reassured. You don't want to go to the hospital. You hate hospitals and doctors. The smell of denatured alcohol nauseates you. Then you think of Alex. Maybe he suffered a concussion. Only the *Post* could make this funny: FAULKNER FRIEND FALLS AFOUL OF FURRY FIEND.

"He's just sleeping off his drunk," Tad says.

"Let's hope."

"Love to be there in the morning when the gang starts coming in for work."

Tad gets some cotton pads and adhesive tape from the medicine cabinet and then cuts some lines on the table while you fuss with the first aid.

With the application of anesthetics, the pain and guilt recede and the episode becomes a source of hilarity. "Giants," Tad says. "Fucking giants. I'm thinking, Who is this dwarf calling me a goddamned pygmy. Then—boom. Fred the Ferret to the rescue. *De casibus virorum illustrium*, as we used to say in Latin class."

"Say what?"

"Something about the fall of famous men."

Tad suggests taking the show on the road. He says it's early yet. You say it's not that early, and he points out that it's not as if you had a job to wake up for in the morning. This is a convincing point. You agree to one drink at Heartbreak.

In the cab on the way downtown, Tad says, "Thanks for taking Vicky off my hands. Inge is eternally grateful."

"My pleasure."

"Really? Got lucky, did you?"

"None of your business."

"Are you serious?" He leans over and looks into your face. "You are serious. Well, well. To each his own."

The cabby swerves between lanes, muttering in a Middle Eastern language.

"Anyway, it's nice to see you getting over this Amanda deal. I mean, she wasn't hard to look at. God knows. But I don't see why you felt like you had to marry her."

"I've been wondering that myself."

"Weren't you suspicious when you saw the sign on her forehead?"

"Which sign was that?"

"The one that said, *Space to Let. Long and Short Term Leasing.*"

"We met in a bar. It was too dark to read."

"Not so dark that she couldn't see you were her ticket out of Trailer Park Land. Bright lights, big city. If you really wanted to do the happy couple thing you shouldn't have let her model. A week on Seventh Avenue would warp a nun. Where skin-deep is the mode, your traditional domestic values are not going to take root and flourish. Amanda was trying to get as far from red dirt and four-wheel drive as she could. She figured out she could trade on her looks farther than she got with you."

For Tad, Amanda's departure was not only not surprising but inevitable. It confirmed his world view. Your heartbreak is just another version of the same old story.

Toward dawn you are riding around in a limo with a guy named Bernie and his two assistants. The assistants are named Maria and Crystal. Crystal is in the back seat with one arm around you and the other around Allagash. Bernie and Maria are facing you from the jump seats. Bernie runs his hand up and down Maria's leg. You're not sure if Tad knew these people before tonight or if they are new friends. Tad seems to think he knows of a party somewhere. Maria says she wants to go to New Chursey. Bernie puts a hand on your knee.

"This is my office," he says. "So what do you think?"

You're not sure you want to know what line of work Bernie is in.

"You got an office like this?"

You shake your head.

"Of course you don't. You got Ivy League written all over you. But I could buy you and your old man and his country club. I use guys like you in your button-down shirts to fetch my coffee."

You nod. You wonder if he's hiring this week and how much it pays.

"You're wondering where the rest of my operation is, right?"

"Not really," you say.

Tad is disappearing inside Crystal's dress.

"You'd like to know, wouldn't you?" Bernie says. "You know what? I'm going to tell you. It's down on the Lower East Side, Avenue D and the Twilight Zone. Not too far from where my old *Bubbie* and *Zadie* ruined their health in a sweatshop so their kids could move out to Scarsdale and Metuchen. It's spics and junkies now. I'll show you. I'll even tell you how we move the product. You want to know?"

"I don't think so."

"Smart. You're a smart boy. I don't blame you

for not wanting to know. You know what happens to people who know too much?"

"What's that?"

"They become Dog Chow. Fucking Purina Dog Chow."

Tad looks up. "We handle that account at the agency."

You ask yourself: How did I get here? The hand that Fred bit throbs painfully. You wonder if it's rabies. You wonder if Alex is all right.

"Used to be," Bernie says, "this was your basic greaseball sector of the economy. You're dealing with your South American spics and your New Jersey dago element. It was an up-and-down scene—all these Latin types with long knives and short tempers—but there was a lot of room for the entrepreneurial spirit. Now we're seeing a different kind of money moving into the neighborhood. I'm talking to three-piece bankers with P.O. boxes in Switzerland. That's one of the things that's happening to this business. But these guys I can deal with. All they want is a good return on their money. Simple. What I'm scared of is my brother Jews—the Hasidim. They're moving in in a big way, crowding out the independent. It's more lucrative than diamonds—hey, they're not stupid. They know an opportunity when they see one. They're all set up for something like this. Liquid capital, world-wide organization, secrecy and trust. How can they lose? I'm telling you, most of the blow in the country already has a Yiddish accent."

"You mean the guys with the black hats and funky sideburns?" Tad says.

"Believe me," Bernie says, "it ain't like they can't afford a haircut. So what do you think of the Yankees this year?"

"Looking good for a pennant," Tad says.

You bail out at the next red light, claiming car sickness. You are halfway up the block when Bernie calls out—"Hey, you! Don't forget. Dog Chow."

O COUTURE!

Your interest in clothing doesn't normally take you beyond Brooks Brothers and J. Press—and at the moment there seems to be a little credit trouble at both establishments. But this morning you are waiting to enter the ballroom of the Waldorf-Astoria, where a fashion designer is showing his fall line. You copped an invitation from your friend at *Vogue*. He owes you for the time he took your Austin Healey out to Westchester and plowed it into a ten-point buck. You know people who have been hunting for twenty years and have never seen ten points on one deer. The car ended up in a junkyard outside of Pleasantville. You don't know what happened to the deer, and it's hard to say what happened to the insurance money except that it was gone in two weeks.

At the door, a tall woman with silver hair scrutinizes your invitation. On either side of the door, two large black men in turbans stand with their arms folded across their chests. They are supposed to be Nubian slaves or something. Only an Italian fashion designer could get away with this. The woman seems to be an ethnic group unto herself. She has no eyebrows or eyelashes and her hairline is extremely high, not far from the top of her skull. Was she in an accident, or is she just chic? She is staring at your homemade bandage, which this season is gray and spotted.

"Mister . . ."

"Allagash," you say, pulling yourself up into military posture. It's the first name that comes to mind. You're not about to use your own.

"From *Vogue*?" she says.

"Since last week."

She nods and returns your invitation. She narrows her eyes and wrinkles her nose as if to say she will feed you to the giant Nubians if you're lying.

You spot the bar and it appears to be open. The veteran department-store buyers are huddled in the vicinity, clutching glasses. They look like they would rather be in Florida. It could be a mistake to start in at the bar right away; indeed, by any reasonable standard of conduct it is a mistake to be here at all, using someone else's name, with a vague notion of disrupting the proceedings.

You excuse your way up to the bar and order vodka. "With ice," you say, when the bartender asks how you want it. "And one for my date," you add.

With your two drinks in your hands, you move away from the bar and strike a determined pose in the middle of the crowd, looking around the room with furrowed brow as if you were searching for your very good friend The Revlon Girl. You don't want to be too conspicuous. There is a slim chance that one of Amanda's friends will recognize you and sic the giant Nubians on you before you have had a chance to do whatever it is you are here to do. This, you realize, is how the terrorist feels as he waits in the crowd with the bomb in his briefcase, believing that everyone can look through a window in his head and see murder on his mind. Your knees are shaky. You drink one of your two drinks. Alas, you would

not make a very good terrorist. Then you remember seeing a briefcase standing beside the
bar and a small flash of cognition, coincident with
the first tingle of alcohol, flickers in your brain.

You walk back to the bar. The briefcase is still
there. The owner appears to be the balding man
with the Bain de Soleil complexion talking to two
Oriental girls. His back is turned to the briefcase.
You lean against the bar on your elbows, looking
bored.

"Can I get you something?" the bartender in-
quires. He frowns when you say no, and you
think there is a trace of suspicion in the way he
looks you over before turning away.

"I don't know how to sail the damn thing," the
balding man says. "I pay some Greeks to do that."
The girls consult, putting their heads together,
and then they laugh. Apparently they took a vote.
He is telling them about islands when you slip
away with the briefcase. *Pas de* sweat.

You take a seat on the near side of the runway,
in the middle of a middle row, thinking that once
the show gets underway you want to be as in-
accessible as possible. You stash the briefcase
under the seat and cover it with your jacket. Your
plan is beginning to congeal.

An eddy in the crowd ripples out from the
door, a sense of waters being parted. Flashbulbs

ignite. Finally you see the cause of the excite-
ment: a face that brings to mind a line of cosmetics, a Cola and recent shocking revelations
in supermarket tabloids. It's the famous actress/
model on a busman's holiday. She's wearing faded
jeans, a sweatshirt and a yachting cap, as if to
say: "I can look terrific with both hands tied behind my back." You know for a fact, or at least
you have it on good authority from Amanda, who
once did location work with her, that she is a
martyr to the search for the perfect nose. She
has had no less than seven reconstructive oper-
ations and she's still not happy. She refuses to
be photographed in profile. You can think of better ways to traumatize the nasal cartilage. From
this distance, the nose looks unexceptional and
the rest strikes you as bland. You judge her to
be about five-five, not tall enough for runway
work. She's got too much chest for couture.

Amanda is, or was, a perfect eight: hips thirty-
four, waist twenty-three, bust thirty-three. You
also know her shoe, glove and ring sizes. Clara
would be proud. You have all the numbers. Fac-
toring in the cheekbones, which a photographer
once described as "neo-classical," they add up to
a hundred and fifty dollars an hour.

People are taking their seats. A woman in a
pink gown comes out onto the runway, appar-

ently the mistress of ceremonies. She smiles and nods, mouthing little greetings, and walks out to the lectern at the runway's edge. Your hands are beginning to shake and you decide on a booster shot. You buck the flow of the crowd and race for the bar. People are looking at you and you are afraid they know your every thought. You brace yourself with the fact that you looked at Amanda every day for almost three years and you don't have the ghost of a clue what was going on in her mind. She showed all the vital signs and made all the right noises. She said she loved you.

The lights are dimmed, and the woman in pink begins to explain the reason we are here today. She says something about a Revolution in Taste. This fashion designer has the same name as a famous Renaissance painter, and she thinks it is not too much to compare the impact of his work in couture with that of the Old Master in painting. Meanwhile, the bartender tells you that the bar is closed until after the show, but he makes an exception for you and your ten-dollar bill. He is about your age. You want to tell him about Amanda. Instead you say, "Lots of jewelry in this crowd. I don't see much in the way of security."

He looks at you. "They're around," he says with conviction. You tell yourself, nice move. You thought that your phrasing cleverly disguised your real interest in the security question, but now he has you pegged for a jewel thief, which in his eyes may be even worse than a sexually abandoned husband. If only your hands would stop shaking. He is looking you over; it is obvious he doesn't like what he sees. He is going to call the Pinkertons, or the giant Nubians, at any minute. They will beat the soles of your feet until you admit everything. Amanda will watch your inglorious exit and think, So this is what he has come to.

"My girlfriend was just a little worried about her necklace," you say to the bartender. "Maybe I should bring her a drink, too, while I'm up."

He doles a few fingers into another glass. "Skip the ice," you say. His look is frosty. "Her husband wouldn't be too thrilled if she came home without her necklace." You wink. "He thinks she's playing bridge." Why are you saying these things?

You look back over your shoulder as you head for your seat. The bartender is signaling someone. You slide past all the knees, apologizing and spilling. The pink lady is talking about Bold New Looks. The first model comes out as you take your seat. She is black and tall as a Zulu. The pink lady describes her outfit, emphasizing the ruffles and their importance to the new elegance.

Amanda is the third model out. At least you think it's Amanda. With the makeup and the pulled-back hair, you can't be absolutely certain. The walk is stylized, but you think you recognize Amanda's signature sway and rhythm. She takes her spin on the runway and then she's gone. You didn't have time to think. You can't decide if it was really her. You remember your friends used to say they had seen her in the *Times* magazine or somewhere when it was actually another model. Sometimes they brought you pictures they had clipped and you would think it was funny—the pictures looked nothing like Amanda. But since she left, you have had the same trouble identifying her face. You have gone back through her portfolio and tried to make a composite that matches the image in your memory. The photos all look slightly different. Her agent said she could do any look—temptress, businesswoman, girl next door. A designer who used her all the time said she had plastic features. You begin to suspect that all of your firm beliefs about Amanda were no more substantial than the images she bodied forth under the klieg lights. You saw what she was selling then; you saw what you wanted to see.

You clutch the edge of your seat and wait for

her next appearance. You have your plan worked out, more or less. You will confront her when she comes out again. If they try to stop you, you will tell them the briefcase is full of high explosives, that you will blow the place into orbit if anybody comes near you. The Zulu comes out again in a new outfit. Then another model. The next one should be Amanda, but it's a brunette. You panic. She has seen you. She won't come out again. But the next model is Amanda, or the woman you think is Amanda. As she advances down the runway, you stand up. The pink lady is enthusing about pleats. You want to shout Amanda's name, but your voice is gone. People are beginning to look at you. A small clicking sound is coming from your throat. Finally you hear your voice: "A-man-da!"

She keeps walking. She walks to the end of the runway and pirouettes in a way that flares the skirt of her dress. She walks down one arm of the T, turns and walks down the other. When she is almost directly in front of you, she turns and looks at you. It is a look that could carry either hatred or indifference. You want to ask for an explanation. She turns away and retraces her steps down the runway as if nothing had happened. Whoever she is, she is a professional. Whoever she is, you don't know her.

The pink lady is asking you to please sit down. People are turning in their seats to look at you. They are saying *Sit down!* and *What does he want?* A photographer up front snaps your picture just in case you turn out to be news. You imagine the *Post*'s caption: SEXUALLY ABANDONED HUBBY GOES BERSERK. Two large men in suits are hurrying down the aisles. The wires hanging from their ears probably connect earplugs with small transmitter-receivers. But it is more interesting to consider the possibility that the men could be robots. How do you know that the terrified-looking woman sitting next to you is actually feeling what you would call terror? If you were to step on her foot she would cry out, but how do you know she would *feel* what you call pain? You could observe one of these robots for years and never know. You could even be married to one.

The robot men are coming down the row of seats to get you, one from either side. You applaud this clever and efficient maneuver. Someone has turned up the music on the sound system, perhaps to cover the noise of your apprehension. You do not resist as one of the men with a wire hanging out of his ear takes your arm and says "Let's go." You follow him down the row of seats and apologize to the people whose knees you are bumping. Once he gets you into the main aisle, he grips your arm uncompromisingly.

The two robots escort you out through the lobby. You are temporarily engulfed by a band of Japanese tourists following a guide with a pink flag and ideographic lapel badge. Your escorts are talking into microphones attached to their sleeves. "Agitator apprehended. Proceeding to lobby." Before shoving you out the door, one of the men leans down and says, "We don't want to see you here again."

It is a blue, sunny day—much too sunny for you, thanks. Fortunately, for once you have not forgotten your Ray-Bans. The lunchtime crowd churns Park Avenue. You expect people to gaze at you, horror-stricken, yet nobody pays any attention. On the corner a fat man in a Yankees cap is selling pretzels from a pushcart. A woman in a fur coat holds her right arm erect, hoping to conjure a taxi. A bus roars past. Cautiously, as if you were entering a swimming pool for the first time in years, you ease yourself into the ranks of pedestrians.

"Things happen, people change," is what Amanda said. For her that covered it. You wanted an explanation, an ending that would assign blame and dish up justice. You considered violence and you considered reconciliation. But what you are left with is a premonition of the way your life will fade behind you, like a book you have read too quickly, leaving a dwindling trail of images and emotions, until all you can remember is a name.

LINGUINE
AND
SYMPATHY

After dark you return to the scene of your former crimes to gather up loose odds and ends. Since the magazine went to press this morning, you can assume everyone will have gone home. You feel strange walking into the building, an infidel penetrating the temple. Your hangover from the Waldorf doesn't help.

As you come out of the elevator on twenty-nine, the first person you see is the Ghost. The elevator doors close behind you.

He stands in the middle of the reception area,

head tilted to one side like a robin listening for worms, and says hello.

You feel compelled to turn around and run. Your mere presence seems shameful, especially after last night. The longer you wait, the harder it becomes to speak. It's as if he's deaf and you're dumb.

"Evening," you say in a weird, flickering voice.

He nods his head. "I'm sorry to hear you're leaving us," he says. "If ever you need a good reference . . ."

"Thank you. Thanks very much."

"Goodbye." He turns and rolls off toward Collating. More than anything yet, this strange encounter makes you feel the sadness of leaving.

You check the mirror at the corner of the hall. Clara's door is closed and dark, as is the door which leads to the secret chambers of the Druid. There's a light on in Fact. You proceed cautiously.

Megan is at her desk. She looks up when you come in, goes back to her reading.

"Remember me?"

"I remember something about a lunch date." She keeps her eyes on her desk.

"Oh, no. I'm sorry."

She looks up. "You're always sorry."

"There was this thing I had to do."

"A sweet young thing?"

"An old thing gone sour."

"I have feelings, too, you know."

"Damn it, I'm sorry."

"I know you've had a lot on your mind lately," Megan says.

"How about dinner?"

"One more meal with you could be the death of me." She's smiling now.

"Just let me pack up my things here. Won't take a minute."

Once you open the drawers of your desk you realize it could take all night. There is a vast quantity of flotsam: files, notebooks, personal and business correspondence, galleys and proofs, review books, matchbooks, loose sheets with names and phone numbers, notes to yourself, first drafts of stories, sketches and poems. Here, for instance, is the first draft of "Birds of Manhattan." Also the "U.S. Government Abstract of Statistics on Agriculture, 1981," indispensable in researching the three-part article on the death of the family farm, and on the back of which you have written the name Laura Bowman and a telephone number. Who is Laura Bowman? You could dial the number and ask for her, ask her where she fits into your past. Tell her you are suffering from amnesia and looking for clues.

In the top drawer you discover two empty rectangular packets. Actually, one of them is not quite empty; inside the black paper is a fine dusting of white. You scrape it onto the desk with a credit card, using the edge of the card to rake up two clean lines. You look over at Megan. She's reading. You could quietly hoover the lines and she'd never know the difference. You extract a bill from your wallet and roll it into a tight cylinder between thumb and forefinger. One apiece isn't going to do much for either of you. On the other hand, two won't do much for you, either; one will make you want another, and another will only initiate a chain reaction of desperate longings. Is this self-knowledge? In any case, you want to do something nice for Megan. For her it might be a treat, something out of the ordinary.

"Meg. Come over here a minute." Now you are committed.

You hold out the bill. She raises her eyebrows.

"This will make you forget you didn't eat lunch."

"What is it?"

"The powder that made Bolivia famous."

She lifts the bill tentatively to her nose and bends over the desk.

"Do the other one, too," you say when she offers you the bill.

"Are you sure?"

"Sure." You just wish she would hurry up and finish it off.

Meg twists her nose like a rabbit and sniffles. "Thanks."

You shovel the contents of the top drawer onto the desk and wonder how, exactly, to deal with all this paper. Some of it may be significant. Most of it is junk. How do you tell the difference?

"We had some trouble here this morning," Megan says. She sits down on the edge of your desk. You resist the urge to jump out of the chair and run down the hall with your jacket pulled over your head. *No comment.* All day you have been stifling the memory of your drunken-commando raid on Clara's office. You want to explain to Megan that it was a joke, you were drunk, it was Tad's idea. It wasn't really you, just a clownish alter ego over whom you have no control. You don't do things like that. You're not that kind of guy at all. If Alex were seriously hurt, though, Meg probably would have said so already. You keep your eyes fixed on a pamphlet entitled "Manual of Factual Verification."

"What do you mean, trouble?"

"Well, when Rittenhouse came in this morning he found Alex Hardy passed out on the floor of Clara's office."

You find it difficult to talk. "Really? Is he all right?"

"I don't imagine he feels terrific. He'll be fine once his blood detoxifies. He's taking the cure up at McLean's. Famous Drinking Writers' Club."

"Didn't he hurt himself when he fell?"

"That's the strange thing. There was no sign of injury, but there was blood on the floor of Clara's office. And on the walls, too. Very peculiar."

"Did he say anything? I mean, about what happened?"

"Nothing coherent. He said something about being attacked by pygmies."

"They didn't call the, uh, police, did they?"

"Why would they?"

"Just wondering. Sounds to me like a weird deal all around." You start to relax. Alex is okay and the visions of cops at your door are fading.

"Another odd thing," Megan says. "There was a mink in the mail room."

"A *mink*?"

"It was hiding in a mail bag full of rejected manuscripts. When the mail guy hoisted the bag this morning it started biting him. They had to call the ASPCA."

"Really strange." Poor Fred, you think.

"How are you coming?" she says, pointing at the desk.

"I think this calls for drastic measures." You stand up and collect all the wastebaskets in the room, lining them up beside the desk. You take a book from the desk and hand it to Megan. "Could you give this to Alex for me? Tell him it's one of the Young Turks." She takes the book. You pull open the drawers one by one and dump the contents, entire, into the steel buckets.

"That's done. Let's eat."

In the cab, you ask Megan where she wants to eat.

"How about my place?"

"You're going to cook?"

"You sound suspicious."

"It just seems like a radical idea."

"If you'd rather go out . . ."

"No. That sounds great."

You get out at Bleecker Street. Megan takes your hand and leads you into a delicatessen. She holds up a box for your approval. "Linguine," she says. You nod. "I'm going to teach you how to purchase and make a meal." In the next aisle she introduces you to two cans of clams. Ordinarily, she says, she would use fresh clams and fresh pasta, but she doesn't want to scare you on your first lesson.

From the deli you walk toward Sixth. Megan is telling you about the difference between fresh and dried pasta. Each step takes you closer to the old apartment on Cornelia Street, where you first lived with Amanda in New York. This was your neighborhood. These shops were your shops. You possessed these streets as securely as if you held title. Now the vista is skewed slightly, someone has tilted the ground a few degrees, and everything is the same and not the same.

You pass Ottomanelli's Meats, where the corpses of small animals hang in the window: unskinned rabbits, hairless fetal pigs, plucked fowl with yellow feet. No ferrets. Amanda was always grossed out by this display. Already she was aspiring to the Upper East Side, where the butchers dress their wares in paper replicas of designer outfits.

At the corner of Jones and Bleecker a Chinese restaurant has replaced the bar whose lesbian patrons kept you awake so many summer nights when, too hot to sleep, you lay together with the windows open. Just before you moved out of the neighborhood a delegation of illiberal youths from New Jersey went into the bar with baseball bats after one of their number had been thrown out.

The lesbians had pool cues. Casualties ran heavy on both sides and the bar was closed by order of the department of something or other.

Farther along, the obese gypsy Madame Katrinka beckons you to enter her storefront parlor with red velvet couch to have your fortune told. What would she have told you a year ago?

"Best bread in the city," Megan says, pointing to Zito's Bakery. The bell over the door rings as you enter. The fragrance of the interior reminds you of mornings on Cornelia when you woke to the smell of bread from the bakery ovens, Amanda sleeping beside you. It seems a lifetime ago, but you can see her sleeping. You just can't remember what you talked about.

"White or wheat," Megan asks.

"I don't know. White, I guess."

"You don't know what's good for you."

"All right, wheat. Wheat's better."

From the bakery you proceed to the vegetable stand. Why are all the vegetables in the city sold by Koreans? Boxes of tumescent produce glisten under the green awning. You wonder if they color-coordinate the displays according to secret Oriental principles of mind control. Maybe they know that the juxtaposition of red tomatoes and yellow squash will produce in the consumer an irresistible urge to buy a bag of expensive oranges. Megan buys fresh basil, garlic, romaine lettuce and tomatoes. "Now *there's* a tomato," she says, holding a large red vegetable up for your inspection. Or is it a fruit?

Megan lives in a big fifties building on Charlton and Sixth. Two large cats, a Siamese and a calico, are waiting at the door. She introduces them as Rosencrantz and Guildenstern: Rose and Guildy for short, explaining that her first off-off-Broadway role was Gertrude in a rock-and-roll version of *Hamlet*.

"I didn't know you were an actress."

"My first love. But I got tired of waitressing."

The apartment is a studio, not large, but furnished to give the impression of distinct areas. Against one wall is a double bed with patchwork quilt. In the center of the room a floral couch and matching chairs are grouped in front of the largest window. At the other end of the room a rolltop desk is sheltered behind a row of bookcases. The tidiness of this arrangement is qualified by strident outbursts of plant life.

The cats stroke themselves on Megan's ankles

while she hangs her shawl in a closet by the door. "How about a glass of wine?" she says.

"Sure. Thanks."

The cats follow her into the kitchen. You read the bookshelves. In the examination of personal libraries is an entire hermeneutics of character analysis. Megan has functional blond maple shelves with a little bit of everything in them. The shelves themselves are just untidy enough to suggest actual use and just neat enough to indicate respect for the equipment. The books are organized according to broad categories: a shelf of poetry, a cluster of oversized art books, a long row of *livre de poche* French novels, music and opera books, scores of thin Samuel French drama scripts, and half a shelf of memoirs of life at the magazine. The latter is an entire genre. You pull out Franklin Woolcraft's chatty volume, *Man about Town;* the flyleaf is signed: "To Meg, who keeps me honest, with Love." Putting the book back, you catch sight of a spine that reads *Exercise for Better Sex.*

Megan returns with two glasses of red wine. "Give me a minute to change," she says. "Then I'm going to teach you how to make the world's easiest meal."

Megan goes over to the freestanding wardrobe

beside the bed. Where is she going to change? Just how casual are we here? As she digs through the wardrobe, you can't help noticing that she has a terrific ass. You have worked with her for almost two years without noticing her ass. How old is she anyway? She removes something from a hanger and tells you she'll be right back. She goes into the bathroom. The Siamese massages its head on your shin. *Exercise for Better Sex.*

Megan comes out wearing a maroon silk shirt with puffed sleeves which is not open to immediate interpretation. One less button buttoned might mean *sexy*, but what you see suggests *casually dressy.*

"Sit down," Megan says, gesturing toward the couch.

You both sit. "I like your place," you say.

"It's small, but I can't afford to move."

You hope the conversation improves. A few minutes ago you were colleagues headed out for a bite to eat. Now you are a man and a woman alone in a room with a bed.

One of the photographs on the end table beside the couch is a large glossy of a younger-looking Megan onstage with two men.

"That was my last play. *Who's Afraid of Virginia Woolf?* in Bridgeport, Connecticut."

You pick up another picture, a boy with a fishing rod holding a trout, cabin and woods in the background.

"Old boyfriend?"

Meg shakes her head. She slides across the couch and takes the picture, studying it earnestly. "My son," she says.

"*Son?*"

Megan nods, looking at the picture. "This was taken a couple of years ago. He's thirteen now. I haven't seen him in almost a year, but he's coming for a visit as soon as school lets out."

You don't want to appear too inquisitive. This sounds like a dangerous subject. You haven't heard about a son before. Suddenly Megan seems much less scrutable than you had imagined.

She reaches across your chest to put the picture back on the end table. You can feel her breath on your cheek.

"He lives with his father in northern Michigan. It's a good place for a boy to grow up. They do boy things—hunting and fishing. His father's a logger. When I met him he was an aspiring playwright who couldn't get his plays produced. It was hard. We were broke and it seemed like everyone else had money. And I wasn't the greatest wife in the world. Jack—that's my ex-husband—didn't want his son growing up in the city.

I didn't want to leave. Of course I didn't want my son to leave either, but when the decision was made I was in Bellevue stupefied with Librium. Obviously in no position to fight for custody."

You don't know what to say. You are embarrassed. You want to hear more. Megan sips her wine and looks out the window. You wonder how painful this is for her.

"Did your husband commit you?"

"He didn't have much choice. I was raving. Manic depression. They finally figured out a few years ago it was a simple chemical deficiency. Something called lithium carbonate. Now I take four tablets a day and I'm fine. But it's a little late to become a full-time mother again. Anyway Dylan—that's my son—has a wonderful stepmother and I see him every summer."

"That's awful," you say.

"It's not so bad. I'm okay now, Dylan has a good life. I call that a good deal. How about some dinner?"

You would rather fill in the gaps of the story, hear all the details, the shrieks and moans of Bellevue, but Megan is up and she is holding out her hand.

In the kitchen she passes you a paring knife and three cloves of garlic which you are supposed to peel. The skin is hard to remove. She explains that it's easier if you whack them a few times with the blunt edge of the knife. Then she notices the bandage. "What happened to your hand?"

"Got caught in a door. No big deal."

Megan goes behind you to wash lettuce in the sink. When you step back to get a better angle on the cutting board your buttocks meet. She laughs.

Megan moves around to the stove. She reaches up to an open shelf and pulls down a bottle. "Olive oil," she says. She pours some in a sauce-pan and turns on the burner. You pour yourself another glass of wine. "Is the garlic ready," Meg asks. You have succeeded in peeling two cloves. They look nude. "Not too efficient, are we?" Megan says. She relieves you of the knife and strips the third clove, then chops it all up. "Now we dump the garlic in the pan and let it fry. Meanwhile, I'll chop the basil while you open the clams. You know how to operate a can opener?"

You mostly stand and watch as Meg flashes around the kitchen. She moves you occasionally, whenever you're in the way. You like the feel of her hands on your shoulders.

"Tell me about Amanda," Megan says over salad. You are sitting at the table in the dining alcove in candlelight. "I get the feeling that something bad happened."

"Amanda is a fictional character," you say. "I made her up. I didn't realize this until recently, when another woman, also named Amanda, shed me with a collect phone call from Paris. Do you mind if I open another bottle of wine?"

You eventually give Megan the gist of it. She says that Amanda must be enormously confused. You will drink to that.

"You've had a terrible time, haven't you?" she says. You shrug. You are looking at her breasts, trying to determine whether or not she is wearing a bra.

"I've been worried about you," Megan says.

You move from the table to the couch. Megan says that we all project our needs onto others, and that others aren't always capable of fulfilling them. No bra, you decide.

You excuse yourself to go to the bathroom. You switch on the light and close the door behind you. The bathroom has a cluttered, homey look. Dried flowers on the toilet tank, white sheepskin on the seat. You pull back the shower curtain. Inside the shower is a shelf loaded with bottles. *Vitabath, Bath & Shower Gelée*. You like the sound of that. *Pantene Shampoo. Pantene Conditioner.* Doubtless this should not make you think of *panties*, but it does. *Lubriderm Lotion.* You pick up a luffa and rub it against your cheek, then return it to the shelf. A pink disposable razor is cradled in the soap dish.

You open the medicine cabinet over the sink: cosmetics, the usual assortment of noneuphoric home medicines. A tube of *Gynol II Contraceptive Jelly. Odorless, Colorless, Flavorless.* This is good news. On the top shelf there is a cache of prescription bottles. You remove one: "Megan Avery; Lithium Carbonate; four tablets daily." The second bottle is tetracycline. So far as you know you are not suffering from bacterial infection. You replace it. You score on the third try: "Valium, as directed, for tension." Tension you've got. You hold the bottle up to the light. Nearly full. After a brief struggle you master the childproof cap. You shake a blue tab onto your palm and swallow it. You consider. The last time you dropped a Valium you didn't even feel it. You take another. Of course, the last time you took a V, you were wired on C. Anyway. You replace the bottle, take an L and flush.

Megan is making noises with the dishes in the kitchen when you return. "Be right out," she says. You sit on the couch and pour another glass from the bottle on the coffee table. A bouquet with a hint of migrant-worker sweat.

"Just thought I'd get the dishes out of the way," Megan says when she returns.

"A good policy," you say. "Want some more wine?"

She shakes her head. "I'm not much of a drinker anymore."

"That's a good policy, too." You are feeling magnanimous.

"Are you doing any writing," Megan asks.

You shrug your shoulders. "I've been working on some ideas."

"Do it," Megan says. "I want to see you walk back into that place someday to pick up a check in Fiction. I want to see you walk past Clara's office into the Department. I'll have a bottle of champagne waiting."

You don't know how Megan has come to believe in you, since you don't even believe in yourself. But you're grateful. You try to picture the scene of your triumphal return to the magazine, but instead you find yourself admiring Megan's bare feet drawn up beside her thighs on the couch.

"What will you do in the meantime? Any job prospects?"

"I've got some leads," you say.

"I could put you in touch with a few people," she says. "What you've got to do is make up a good résumé—wide enough for journalism and publishing. I know an editor at Harper & Row who'd be happy to talk to you. I've already talked to Clara, and she says as far as the magazine is concerned, the parting was amicable and you'll get a good recommendation."

You appreciate Megan's wonderful efficiency, but getting fired really wore you out and you would just as soon put the question of new employment on hold. Right now you would like to drink some more of this wine and sink a little deeper into the upholstery. You would like to show Megan how grateful you are. You reach over and take her hand. "Thanks," you say.

"And don't be afraid to ask for a loan to tide you over."

"You're terrific."

"I just want to help you get back on your feet."

Not now, you think. You'd rather lie down. Bury your head in Megan's lap and stay there for a week or two. The bed is just a few feet away. You lean over and place your free hand on Megan's shoulder. The silk slides back and forth across her skin as you massage. No bra strap. You look into her eyes. She's a rare woman. She smiles, reaches out and strokes your hair.

"Everything's going to work out," she says.

You nod.

Her face registers a shift of thought, and then she says, "How's your father doing?"

"He's fine," you say. "He's terrific." You pull her toward you. You slide a hand behind her head and close your eyes as your lips find hers. You press her head against the back of the couch and run your tongue along her teeth. You want to feel her tongue. You want to disappear inside her mouth. She turns her head away and tries to withdraw from your embrace. You reach a hand under her shirt. Gently, she grips your hand and holds it there.

"No," she says. "That's not what you want." Her voice is calm and soothing. She is not angry, just determined. When you try to advance your hand she stops it.

"Not that," she says. When you try to kiss her again she holds you off, but she remains on the couch. You feel like water seeking its own level, and Megan is the sea. You put your head in her lap. She strokes your hair. "Calm down," she says. "Calm down."

■

"Are you all right now," Megan asks when you lift your head from her lap.

The level of the room keeps changing. All of the surfaces swell and recede with oceanic rhythm. You are not quite all right. You are somewhat wrong.

"I think maybe I'll get up and go to the, uh, bathroom." This is you speaking. Testing: one, two, three.

Megan is helping you to your feet. She holds your elbow as she leads you to the door. "I'll be right out here if you need me."

The black-and-white tiles on the floor keep moving. You stand in front of the toilet and consider. Do you feel sick? Not exactly. Not yet, anyway. You might as well take a leak, though, as long as you are here. You unzip and aim for the bowl. There is a poster with some kind of print in front of you. You lean forward to read it, and then you lean back, so as not to fall forward.

You try to grab hold of the shower curtain as you go down but you can't get a grip.

"Are you all right?" Megan says from the other side of the door.

"Fine," you say. You are mostly in the tub. Only your feet stick out, way down at the far end of your body. It's not uncomfortable, really, except that you are a little damp around the midsection. You will have to investigate this. Find the source. In a minute.

The door opens. Help is on the way.

SOMETIMES
A
VAGUE
NOTION

You wake up with a cat on your chest. You are on a couch, wrapped in a quilt. After a few minutes you recognize Megan's apartment. Her bed is empty. The clock on the nightstand says 11:13. That would be A.M., judging by the sunlight. The last thing you remember is an amorous lunge at Megan somewhere in the P.M.; presumably unsuccessful. You have the feeling you have made a fool out of yourself.

You sit up in bed and marvel at this strange pair of pajamas. You stand up. There is a note on the kitchen table: *Eggs, English muffins and orange juice in fridge. Your clothes are hanging in bathroom. Give a call later on. Love—Megan.*

At least she doesn't hate you. Perhaps you did not entirely disgrace yourself. Better not to think about it. You find your clothes in the bathroom. Everything is stiff and clean as if freshly laundered. The calico cat jumps up on the sink and rubs its head on your hip as you dress.

You should leave a note for Meg. You find a pen and a fat pad in which every sheet has MEMO written across the top.

Dear Meg—Thanks for the bed and board. Dinner was delicious. Now what? Should you acknowledge loss of full recall? *I guess I nodded off a little early.* The question is, what did you do before that? For that matter, what about after? What you need is an all-purpose apology. Something to cover each possible misdemeanor. *Please excuse my lapse from gentlemanly comportment. Let's get together soon, maybe for lunch.*

You rip this up. On the new sheet you write: *Dear Megan—I'm sorry. I know I'm always saying that, but I mean it. Thank you.*

The phone is ringing when you get back to your apartment. Living dangerously, you answer. It's Richard Fox, the reporter. He says he heard a rumor about your recent loss of employment. He says he liked a book review you wrote for the *Village Voice* a while back. Nobody reads book reviews in the *Voice*, but you admire the diligence exhibited by Fox's assistant in tracking the thing down. He mentions an opening at *Harper's* that might be right for you, and says that he could put in a good word. He is too kind. He wasn't nearly so friendly when you met him at the publication party for his last book.

"I met Clara Tillinghast a few weeks ago," he says. "No man I'd care to drink with could put up with that for long. My sources tell me she had it in for you from the start."

"Short honeymoon, long divorce."

"Would it be accurate to say that she is something of a bitch on wheels?"

"I think she has treads, actually. Like a Sherman tank. But it would be a tough thing to verify."

"I guess you know I'm writing a piece on the magazine."

"Really?"

"I was hoping you might be able to give me some background. You know—human interest, anecdotes."

"You want smut?"

"Whatever you've got."

A baby cockroach is working its way up the wall next to the phone. Should you crush it or let it pass?

"I was just a little worker bee. I don't think I could tell you anything of national interest."

"Let's face it. The stagehands have the best view in the house."

"It's a pretty dull place," you say. Already it seems so far behind you, the office politics and the broom-closet affairs no more interesting there than elsewhere.

"Why feel loyal to them? They threw you out on your ass."

"The whole subject just bores me."

"Let's have lunch. Bat some ideas around. Say, Russian Tea Room at one-thirty?"

You tell him you don't have any ideas. Your information is imperfect. Everything you thought you knew turned out to be wrong. You tell him you are an unreliable source. He appeals to the public's right to know. He appeals to your sense of vengeance. He gives you his phone number in case you change your mind. You don't write it down.

You go out for a bite and the *Post*. It's almost two o'clock. Not for the first time, you wonder why all the coffee shops in the city are run by Greeks. The take-out cups have pictures of semi-nude classical Greek figures.

O Attic shape . . . of paper men and maidens overwrought . . .

You spread the newspaper out on the counter and learn that Coma Baby was delivered six weeks premature in an emergency Caesarean and that Coma Mom is dead.

Coming up West Twelfth from Seventh Avenue you see someone sitting on the steps of your apartment building. It looks an awful lot like your brother Michael. Whoa! You slow down. Then you stop. It is Michael. What is he doing here? He should be home in Bucks County. He doesn't belong here.

He sees you. He stands up, starts toward you. You turn and bolt. The subway entrance is half a block up. You take the steps two at a time, dodging the zombies trudging up the stairs. An uptown train with open doors waits at the platform. A line at the token booth. You vault the turnstile. A metallic voice issues from the speaker on the booth: "Hey, *you!*" You dash inside as the doors close. People are staring. When the train begins to move they return to their *Posts* and their private sorrows.

Looking out the sooty windows at the receding platform and seeing Michael standing outside the turnstiles, you duck away from the window. You don't want to see him. It's not that he's a bad guy. You feel guilty of everything. Even now, a transit cop with a walkie-talkie may be striding through the cars to arrest you.

You sit down and allow the racket of the train to fill your head. You close your eyes. Soon the noise doesn't seem like noise and the motion doesn't feel like motion. You could fall asleep.

You open your eyes and look at the ads. TRAIN FOR AN EXCITING NEW CAREER. BE AN INSTANT WINNER WITH WINGO! SOFT AND LOVELY HAIR RELAXER. BE A MODEL—OR JUST LOOK LIKE ONE.

At Fiftieth you get off and walk up the stairs to the street. Walking east, you cross abrupt thermoclines as you move between the cool shadows of tall buildings and brief regions of direct sunlight. At Fifth Avenue you stand on the corner and look over at the long row of windows fronting Saks. You cross the street to the third window down from the uptown corner.

The mannequin is gone. You count windows again. Where the Amanda mannequin had been is a new one with brunette acrylic on its head and a delicately upturned nose. You walk up and down the block, examining each of the manne- quins. For a moment you think you have found it on Fiftieth Street, but the face is too angular and the nose is wrong.

You came here with a notion of demonstrating to yourself that the icon was powerless, yet you are unsettled now that it is gone. What does this mean? You decide that it has disappeared be- cause you were through with it, and you consider this a good omen.

❑

On Madison you pass a construction site, walled in by acres of plywood on which the faces of various rock stars and Mary O'Brien McCann are plastered. Thirty stories above you, a crane dan- gles an I-beam over the street beside the skeleton of a new building. From the sidewalk the crane looks like a toy, but a few months back you read about a pedestrian who was killed at this site when a cable broke. DEATH FALLS FROM SKY, the *Post* said.

You pass the Helmsley Palace—the shell of old New York transparently veiling the hideous erection of a real estate baron. A camera crew has taken over the sidewalk beside the entrance.

Pedestrians submit to a woman with a clipboard who orders them to detour out into the street. "Close-up with the mini-cam," someone says. The crew wear their importance like uniforms. Out in the bus lane, a kid in a Blessed Mother High School sweatshirt turns down the volume on his ghetto-blaster. "Who is it," he asks you. When you shake your head he turns the music back up.

> Facts are simple and facts are straight
> Facts are lazy and facts are late
> Facts all come with points of view
> Facts don't do what I want them to

"Here she comes," a voice shouts.

You keep walking, thinking briefly about the Missing Person, the one who's come and gone for good. Out into the sunlight of Fifth Avenue and the Plaza, a gargantuan white chateau rising in the middle of the island like a New Money dream of the Old World. When you first came to the city you spent a night here with Amanda. You had friends to stay with, but you wanted to spend that first night at the Plaza. Getting out of the taxi next to the famous fountain, you seemed to be arriving at the premiere of the movie which was to be your life. A doorman greeted you at the steps. A string quartet played in the Palm

Court. Your tenth-floor room was tiny and over-looked an airshaft; though you could not see the city out the window, you believed that it was spread out at your feet. The limousines around the entrances seemed like carriages, and you felt that someday one would wait for you. Today they put you in mind of carrion birds, and you cannot believe your dreams were so shallow.

You are the stuff of which consumer profiles —American Dream: Educated Middle-Class Model—are made. *When you're staying at the Plaza with your beautiful wife, doesn't it make sense to order the best Scotch that money can buy before you go to the theater in your private limousine?*

You stayed there once before, with your parents and your brothers, when your father was in between corporate postings. You and Michael rode the elevators up and down all day. The next day you were going to embark for England on the *Queen Elizabeth*. You told Michael that they didn't have silverware in England, that people had to eat with their hands. Michael started to cry. He didn't want to go to England, didn't want to eat with his hands. You told him not to worry. You would sneak some silverware into the country. Prowling the halls, you stole silverware from the room-service trays and stashed it in your suit-cases. Michael wanted to know if they had glasses. You packed some just in case. At customs in Liverpool Michael began to cry again. You had warned him of the terrible penalties for smuggling. He didn't want to have his hands cut off. A few years ago you were home for the weekend and you found one of the spoons with the Plaza crest in the silverware drawer.

You walk up Fifth Avenue along the park. On the steps of the Metropolitan Museum, a mime with a black-and-white face performs in front of a small crowd. As you pass you hear laughter and when you turn around the mime is imitating your walk. He bows and tips his hat when you stop. You bow back and throw him a quarter.

At the ticket window you say you're a student. The woman asks you if you have an ID. You say you left it in your dorm and she ends up giving you the student rate anyway.

You go to the Egyptian wing and wander among the obelisks, sarcophagi and mummies. In your several visits to the Met this is the only exhibit you have seen. Mummies of all sizes are included, some of them unwrapped to reveal the leathery half-preserved dead. Also dog and cat mummies, and an infant mummy, an ancient newborn bundled up for eternity.

From the Met you walk to Tad's place on Lexington. It's a little after six. No answer to the buzzer. You decide to go for a drink and come back later. In a few minutes you are in singles' heaven on First Avenue. You start at Friday's, where you get a seat at the bar and finally succeed in ordering a drink. Prime time approaches, and the place is packed with eager secretaries and slumming lawyers. Everyone here has the Jordache look—the look you don't want to know better. Hundreds of dollars' worth of cosmetics on the women and thousands in gold around the necks of the open-shirted men. Gold crucifixes, Stars of David and coke spoons hang from the chains. Some trust in God to get them laid; others in drugs. Someone should do a survey of success ratios, publish it in *New York* magazine.

You are sitting beside a girl with frosted hair who emanates the scent of honeysuckle. She has been sneaking peeks at you in between conferences with her girlfriend. You would guess her age to be somewhere in the illegal range. Underneath her eyes she has painted two purple streaks suggestive of cheekbones. You know what's coming, it's only a matter of time. You don't know how to respond. You catch the eye of the bartender and order another drink.

"Excuse me," the girl says. "Do you happen to know where we could get some coke?"

"No can do."

"I do," she says. "I mean, we know where we can score a gram but we don't have enough bread. You wanna go in with us, maybe? We got some ludes."

You are not this desperate, you tell yourself. You still have some self-respect.

You wake to the voice of Elmer Fudd. "Kill the wabbit! Kill the wabbit!" You feel like a murder victim yourself. Then you see a girl with frosted hair and puffy eyes looking down at you and you wonder if the crime isn't rape.

"What happened?"

"Nothing," she says. "Not a goddamn thing. Story of my life. Meet a guy at a bar and carry him home so he can pass out on my bed."

This account of events relieves a fraction of the pain in your head. You are in a strange bed. A television shows the cartoon on the other side of the room. You discover that you are still partially clothed.

"At least you didn't puke," she says.

"You better hope your luck holds."

"Say what?"

"Where am I?"

"You're in my goddamn apartment."

"Where might that be?"

"Queens."

"You're kidding."

"What's to kid?" Her face softens and she strokes your forehead. "You wanna try again?"

"What time is it?" you say. "I'm late for work."

"Cool your jets. It's Saturday."

"I work Saturdays." You sit up in bed, extracting her hand from your hair. You feel ravaged. On the television screen, Wile E. Coyote is building an improbable contraption to catch the Road Runner. Posters on the wall depict rock groups in lurid light and kittens in soft focus.

You hear sounds coming from the next room. "Who's that?" you say, pointing at the door.

The girl is putting a record on the turntable.

"My parents," she says.

By the time you get back to Manhattan it is two o'clock. You feel as if you have come across oceans and mountains. The parents were watching television when you finally worked up the courage to slouch out of the bedroom. They didn't even look up.

You have never been so glad to see the inside of your apartment. You check the refrigerator for liquids. The milk is sour. You are trying to nod off on the couch when the buzzer rings.

When you punch the Listen button a voice says "United Parcel Service." Possibly some kind soul has sent you a brand-new mail-order heart. The voice sounds like it is coming through layers of cloth. Where the hell is the doorman? Does UPS deliver on Saturday? Do you care? You press the Door button and go back to the couch. When the bell rings you go to look through the peephole. Michael is standing in the hall, greatly reduced in size but no less menacing. You consider the fire escape. He steps forward and pounds on the door. The fisheye peephole makes his fist seem like a monstrous appendage. Maybe if you're quiet he'll go away. He pounds again.

You open the door. Michael seems to fill the entire frame.

"Michael," you say. You meet his eyes, which are implacable, then you look down at his feet, on which there are a pair of genuine work boots of a type not usually seen in the city.

You leave the door open and walk back to the living room. He doesn't follow immediately. Presently he enters and slams the door. You stretch out on the couch. "Take a seat," you say. He remains standing in front of you. This is not really fair, you think, aggravating, as it does, his advantage in height.

"What the hell is going on with you?" he says. He is growing larger by the minute.

You shrug.

"I've been trying to track you down for over a week. I called your office, called here."

"When did you get to the city," you ask.

"And then when I take the goddamn bus down to the city and stake out your doorstep, you bolt when you see me."

"I thought you were somebody else."

"Don't give me that shit. I left about a hundred and fifty messages at your office. And then yesterday I go to your office and they tell me you are no longer employed as of Wednesday. What the fuck is going on?" His fists are clenched. You would think it was *his* job you had lost.

"What did you want to see me about?"

"*I* don't *want* to see you. I'd just as soon leave you here to drown in coke or whatever it is you're doing. But Dad's worried about you and I'm worried about Dad."

"How *is* Dad?"

"Do you care?"

You have always thought that Michael would make a great prosecuting attorney. He has an acute sense of universal guilt and a keen nose for circumstantial evidence. Although he is a year younger than you, he has appropriated the role of elder. He takes your foibles and lapses from good citizenship as personal affronts.

"Dad's in California on business. At least he was until last night. He asked me to call and make sure you got home for the weekend. Since you never answer or call back, well, here I am. You're coming home with me whether you want to or not."

"Okay."

"Where are you keeping the Healey?" he says.

"Little problem there. A friend of mine totaled it."

"You let some guy wreck your car?"

"Actually, I told him just to put a few dents in it but he got carried away."

He shakes his head and sighs. He has learned to expect no better from you. Finally he takes a seat, a good sign. He looks around the apartment, which he has never seen before, and shakes his head at the mess. Then he looks at you.

"Tomorrow is the anniversary, in case you've forgotten. One year. We're going to spread her ashes in the lake. Dad wants you to be there."

You nod your head. You knew this was coming. You weren't watching the calendar but you could feel it coming on. You close your eyes and lean your head back against the couch. You surrender.

"Where's Amanda?" he says.

"Amanda?" You open your eyes.

"Your wife. Tall, blond, slender."

"She's shopping," you say.

For what seems like a long time you sit across from each other in silence. You think of your mother. You try to remember the way she was before she got sick.

"You've just forgotten Mom completely, is that it?"

"Don't get righteous with me."

"And Dad, who you haven't seen since Christmas."

"How about if you just shut up."

"You never had to exert yourself for anything and you're not about to start now. School, girls, awards, fancy jobs—it all just falls in your lap, doesn't it? You don't even have to go out and look for it. Mom and Dad certainly couldn't do enough for you. So I guess it gets pretty easy to take people for granted when you're Mr. Everything."

"Omniscience must be a terrible burden, Michael. How do you bear it?"

"Mr. Wonderful, who galloped in from New York last year like some kind of fucking knight in his British sports car, just in time for the dramatic finale of Mom's life. Like it was some goddamn New York party that you didn't want to be early for, God forbid."

"Shut up."

"Don't tell me to shut up."

"How about if I make you shut up?"

You stand up. Michael stands up.

"I'm getting out of here," you say. You turn away. You can hardly see your way to the door. Your eyes are dim and cloudy. You hit your knee on a chair.

"You're not going anywhere."

Michael grabs your arm as you reach the door. You yank it away. He slams you against the doorframe and bangs your head against the metal.

He's got you pinned. You jam your elbow into his belly and he lets go. You turn and punch him in the face. You punch him hard. You hit him with the hand the ferret bit and it hurts like hell. You fall backward into the hall. You get to your feet and look to see what's happened to Michael. He is on his feet. You remember thinking, *He's going to hit me.*

When you come around, you are stretched out on the couch. Your head feels truly awful. You can feel the point of contact just below your left temple.

Michael comes out of the kitchen holding a paper towel to his nose. The towel is stained with blood.

"You all right," you ask him.

He nods. "That kitchen faucet needs a washer. Drips like crazy."

"Amanda isn't shopping," you say. "She left me."

".What?"

"She called up from France one day and said she wasn't coming home."

Michael scrutinizes your face to see if you are

serious. Then he leans back in the chair and sighs.

"I don't <u>know</u> what to say," he says. He shakes his head. "Goddamn. I'm sorry. I'm really sorry."

Michael stands up and comes over to the couch. He crouches down, then says, "Are you all right?"

"I miss Mom," you say.

THE
NIGHT
SHIFT

Michael is hungry and you are thirsty;
a foray is proposed and seconded. All of uptown
seems to be headed downtown for Saturday night.
Everyone on the sidewalk looks exactly seventeen years old and restless. At Sheridan Square
a ragged figure is tearing posters off the utility
poles. He claws at the paper with his fingernails
and then stomps it under his feet.

"What is he, political?" Michael says.

"No, just angry."

You walk down into the Lion's Head, past all

the framed dust jackets of all the writers who have ever gotten drunk here, heading for the back room where the lights are low. When you sit down, James, long-haired and black, jumps up on the table; the house cat.

"I never really liked her much, to tell you the truth," Michael says. "I thought she was fake. If I ever see her I'm going to rip her lungs out."

You introduce Michael to Karen, the waitress, and she asks you how the writing is going. You order two double vodkas. She tosses down a couple of menus and ducks around the corner.

"At first," you say, "I couldn't believe she left me. Now I can't believe we got married in the first place. I'm just starting to remember how cold and distant Amanda was when Mom got sick. She seemed to resent Mom's dying."

"Do you think you'd have married her if Mom hadn't been sick?"

You have made such a point of not dwelling on the incidents associated with your mother's death, almost denying that it was a consideration at all. You were living with Amanda in New York and marriage wasn't high on your list of priorities, although on Amanda's it was. You had your doubts about in sickness and in health till death do us part. Then your mother was diagnosed and everything looked different. Your first love had given notice of departure and Amanda's application was on file. Mom never said it would do her heart good to see you married, but you were so eager to please her you would have walked through fire, given your right and left arms . . . You wanted her to be happy and she wanted you to be happy. And, in the end, you might have confused what she wanted with what Amanda wanted.

Before it happened you couldn't believe you would survive your mother's death. Torn between thinking it was your duty to throw yourself on her pyre and her wish that you should not waste time mourning, you knew no reaction that satisfied both conditions. You spent so much time in anticipation that when her death came you didn't know what you felt. After the funeral it seemed as if you were wandering around your own interior looking for signs of life, finding nothing but empty rooms and white walls. You kept waiting for the onset of grief. You are beginning to suspect it arrived nine months later, disguised as your response to Amanda's departure.

Michael orders the shepherd's pie. You wave the menu away. You talk about the past and the present. You ask about the twins, Peter at Amherst and Sean at Bowdoin. Having already discussed your travails at the magazine, including your recent ferret gambit, you ask Michael about his business—restoring old houses—and he tells you it's going well. He's working on a derelict carriage house in New Hope.

"I'm going to hire out some grunt work. Maybe you'd be interested. At least it's a change of scene. Say, three or four weeks of work."

You tell him you'll think about it. You are surprised that he would offer. Michael has long considered you incompetent. By the time he was twelve he was bigger than you. He shaped an ethic of engagement with the physical world under which your aptitudes and accomplishments were suspect.

You drink and talk. Under the spell of alcohol your differences recede. You and Michael and Peter and Sean and Dad stand against the world. The family has been fucked over, but you're going to tough it out. Forget that slut Amanda. The doctors who couldn't save your mother's life and wouldn't tell you what was going on. Clara Tillinghast. The priest who, at your mother's deathbed, said, "We've seen some beautiful deaths with cancer."

After many drinks Michael says, "I need a little air." On the way back to the apartment, you stop in on a friend who happens to have a spare half for the low, low price of sixty dollars. You feel that you are basically through with this compulsion. This time you just want to celebrate crossing the hump. You are a little drunk and you want to keep going, keep talking.

You should have told us, Michael says, sprawled out on the couch in your apartment. "I mean, what's a family for?" He bangs his hand on the coffee table for emphasis. "What's family for?"

"I don't know. You want to do a few lines?"

Michael shrugs. "Why not?" He watches as you get up and take the mirror from the wall. "What was bad for me," he says, "is at first I'd see her the way she was toward the end, all wasted and thin. But now I have this image I keep with me. I don't know when it was, but I came home from school one day—this was after you'd gone to college—and Mom was out back raking leaves. It was October or something and she was wearing your old ski team jacket, which was about six sizes too big." He stops. His eyes are closed and you think maybe he has passed out. You shake some coke out onto the mirror. Michael opens his eyes. "I remember the way the air smelled, the way Mom looked in that jacket with leaves in her hair, the lake in the background. That's the way I remember her now. Raking leaves in your old Andover ski team jacket."

"I like that," you say. You can imagine it. She wore that jacket for years. Once you finished high school you didn't want any part of it and she took it up. You'd never really given it a thought, but now you feel good about it.

You cut eight lines. Michael begins to snore. You call his name and then you get up and gently shake his shoulder. He turns his face into the cushions. You do two of the lines and sit back in the chair. A year ago tonight you were up until daybreak, sitting beside your mother's bed.

❑

You thought you would faint when you came home the last time, three days before she died, and saw the ravaged form. Even the smile had shifted. After months of waffling, the doctors had admitted there was not much they could do, and agreed she could stay at home if the family would attend her constantly. When you got home, Michael and your father, who had traded twelve-hour shifts for a week, were exhausted. For the last seventy-two hours, you took the night shift, midnight to eight. You gave her the morphine injection every four hours, and tended as best you could to the symptoms of the disease.

When you first saw her, even after Michael had warned you, you wanted to run away. But the horror passed, and you were glad you could do something for her. You were glad you could be with her. But for those last hours you might never have really known her. The last few nights she was not sleeping at all, so you talked.

"Have you ever tried cocaine," she asked that last night.

You didn't know what to say. A strange question from a mother. But she was dying. You said you had tried it.

"It's not bad," she said. "When I could still swallow they were giving me cocaine with morphine. To ease the depression. I liked it."

Your mother, who never smoked a cigarette in her life, who got loopy on two drinks.

She said the morphine was good for the pain but made her drowsier than she wanted to be. She wanted to be clear. She wanted to know what was happening.

Then she said, "Do young men need sex?"

You asked what she meant by *need*.

"You know what I mean. I should know these

things. I don't have much time and there's so much I've always wondered about. I was brought up to think sex was an ordeal that married women had to endure. It took me a long time to get over that idea. I feel sort of cheated."

You always thought your mother was the last Puritan.

"Have you slept with a lot of girls?"

"Mom, really," you said.

"Come on. What's to hide? I wish I'd known a long time ago that I was going to die. We could've gotten to know each other a lot better. There's so much we don't know."

"Okay, there have been some girls."

"Really?" She lifted her head up from the pillow.

"Mother, I'm not going into details."

"Why not?"

"It's, well, embarrassing."

"I wish people wouldn't waste their time being embarrassed. I wish I hadn't. So tell me what it's like."

You began to forget the way she looked then, and to see her somehow as young, younger than you had ever known her. The wasted flesh seemed illusory. You saw her as a young woman.

"Do you really enjoy it," she asked.

"Sure. Yeah, I do."

"You've slept with girls you're not in love with. Isn't it different if you're in love?"

"Sure, it's better."

"How about Sally Keegan? Did you sleep with her?"

Sally Keegan was your high school prom date. "Once."

"I *thought* so." This verification of her intuition pleased her. "What about Stephanie Bates?"

Later, she said, "Are you happy with Amanda?"

"Yes, I think so."

"For the rest of your life?"

"I hope so."

"I was lucky," Mom said. "Your dad and I *have* been happy. But it hasn't always been easy. One time I thought I was leaving him."

"Really?"

"We were human." She adjusted her pillow and winced. "Foolish." She smiled.

The candor was infectious. It spread back to the beginning of your life. You tried to tell her, as well as you could, what it was like being you. You described the feeling you'd always had of being misplaced, of always standing to one side of yourself, of watching yourself in the world even as you were being in the world, and wondering if this was how everyone felt. That you always believed that other people had a clearer idea of what they were doing, and didn't worry quite so much about why. You talked about your first day of school. You cried and clutched her leg. You even remembered how her plaid slacks felt, the scratchiness on your cheek. She sent you off to the bus—she interrupted here to say she wasn't much happier than you were—and you hid in the woods until you saw the bus leave and then went home and told her you had missed it. So Mom drove you to school, and by the time you got there you were an hour late. Everybody watched you come in with your little note, and heard you explain that you missed the bus. When you finally sat down you knew that you would never catch up.

"Don't you think everyone feels a little like that?" Then Mom told you she knew all along about the hot-water-on-the-thermometer trick, but let you pretend you were sick whenever you really seemed to need it. "You were a funny boy. An awful baby. A real screamer." Then she grimaced and for a moment you thought it was the memory of your screaming.

You asked her if she wanted the morphine and she said not yet. She wanted to talk, to be clear.

The window behind the headboard showed a glimmer of gray. In the other rooms your three brothers, your father, and your Aunt Nora were sleeping. Amanda was in New York.

"Was I worse than Michael and the twins?"

"Much worse." She smiled as if she had just conferred a great distinction upon you. "Much, much worse." The smile twisted into a grimace and she clutched the sheet in her fingers.

You begged to give her some morphine. The spasm passed and you saw her body relax.

"Not yet," she said.

She told you how unbearable you were as an infant, always throwing up, biting, crying through the night. "You've never been much good at sleeping, have you? Some nights we had to take you out in the car and drive around to get you to sleep." She seemed pleased. "You were something else."

She winced again and groaned. "Hold my hand," she said. You gave her your hand and she gripped it harder than you would have imagined she could. "The pain," she said.

"Please let me give you that shot."

You couldn't stand to see her suffer much longer, felt you were about to collapse. But she told you to wait.

"Do you know what this is like?" she said. "This pain?"

You shook your head. She didn't answer for a while. You heard the first bird of morning.

"It's like when you were born. It sounds crazy, but that's exactly what it's like."

"It hurt that much?"

"Terrible," she said. "You just didn't want to come out. I didn't think I'd live through it." She sucked breath through her teeth and gripped your hand fiercely. "So now you know why I love you so much." You were not sure you understood, but her voice was so faint and dreamy that you didn't want to interrupt. You held her hand and watched her eyelids flicker, hoping she was dreaming. Birds were calling on all sides. You didn't think you had ever heard so many birds.

In a little while she started to talk again. She described a morning in a two-room apartment over a garage in Manchester, New Hampshire. "I was standing in front of a mirror as if I'd never really seen my own face before." You had to lean down close to hear. "I felt strange. I knew something had happened, but I didn't know what."

She drifted off. Her eyes were half-open but

you could see she was looking somewhere else. The bedroom window was filling with light.

"Dad," she said. "What are you doing here?"

"Mom?"

She was silent for a time and then, suddenly, her eyes were wide open. Her grip relaxed. "The pain is going away," she said.

You said that was good. The light seemed to have entered the room all at once.

"Are you still holding my hand," she asked.

"Yes. I am."

"Good," she said. "Don't let go."

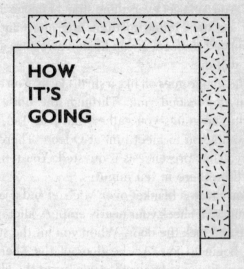

HOW
IT'S
GOING

The apartment has become very small. Michael snores on the couch. Your head is pounding with voices of confession and revelation. You followed the rails of white powder across the mirror in pursuit of a point of convergence where everything was cross-referenced according to a master code. For a second, you felt terrific. You were coming to grips. Then the coke ran out; as you hoovered the last line, you saw yourself hideously close-up with a rolled twenty sticking out of your nose. The goal is receding. Whatever it was. You can't get everything straight in one night. You are too excited to think any more and too exhausted to sleep. If you lie down you are afraid you will die.

The phone goes off like a shrill alarm. You catch it on the second ring. Through the noise and cryptic epigrams you gather that it is Tad, that he wants you to meet him at Odeon. There is a party. Your presence is requested. You tell him you'll be there in ten minutes.

You throw a blanket over Michael and a jacket on yourself; check your nearly empty wallet, then close and lock the door. When you hit the street you begin to jog. At the door of the Sheridan Square all-hours bank office you insert the plastic card which a sign tells you is your passport to banking convenience. When the buzzer sounds, you pull the door open and step into a room the color of an illuminated swimming pool. A specimen in camouflage combat gear stands at the cash-machine as if he were playing a video game, body English in his every motion. If he doesn't hurry up, you think, I will have to kill him.

Finally he turns to you and throws up his hands. "Fucking computers. They ain't gonna take over the world at this rate. This goddamned Citibank unit—it couldn't take Staten Island on a Sunday morning. Go ahead, try your luck." This neo-guerrilla sports a button which reads: I'M NOT AS THINK AS YOU STONED I AM.

Not at all confident that your fellow late-night Citibanker is capable of operating the equipment, you preserve the hope of imminent cash. You step up and read the message on the screen, which welcomes you in Spanish and English and asks you which language you prefer to do your banking in. You decide on English; nothing happens. You press the button again. Eventually you try all of the buttons on the console, which keeps flashing the same hearty greeting. You are not the kind of person who beats on recalcitrant vending machines. Nevertheless, just this once, you would like to put your fist through the video screen. You jam the buttons down into their sockets, raise your foot and uselessly kick the wall. Words vile and violent pass your lips. You hate banks. You hate machines. You hate the idiots outside on the sidewalk.

With your last five you stake yourself to a cab. You begin to feel better once you're in motion.

As you pull up to Odeon, Tad is coming out the door with his friend Jimmy Q from Memphis. Luckily, Jimmy has a limo. You climb in. Jimmy gives the driver an address. The Caddy floats over the downtown streets. You can tell you are moving only by the passage of lights across the tinted windows. Some of the lights have dim halos and others spill crystalline shards into the night.

The car stops in front of a warehouse. You hear the party throbbing like a helicopter above the deserted street. You can't wait to get up there. You drum your fingers on the doorframe as you wait for the elevator.

"Take it easy," Tad says. "You're wired to detonate."

You ask whose party it is. Tad provides a name he claims belongs to the heir of a fast-food fortune.

The elevator door opens directly into the loft, which is roughly the size of a Midwestern state and at least as populous. There are windows on three sides and mirrors on the fourth. A bar and buffet is set up at one end. The dance floor is down at the other end, somewhere near New Jersey.

At the bar, Tad introduces you to a woman, Stevie, who wears a slinky black gown with a scalloped hemline. She is very tall. Long blond hair, tasseled white silk scarf wrapped around her neck. Stevie says, "Do you dance?"

"You bet."

You take Stevie's hand and make for the dance floor, where you add yourselves to the confusion. Elvis Costello says pump it up when you don't really need it. Stevie carves sinuous figures between the beat. You do your patented New York Torque. The music is just about loud enough to drive everything between your ears down through the spinal column into your bones, and possibly you can shake it out via your fingertips, femurs and toes.

Stevie puts her arms on your shoulders and kisses you. When she says she has to go to the Ladies', you head for the bar to get drinks.

Tad awaits you. "Have you seen our friend?"

"Which friend?"

"Your formerly deceased not-yet-ex wife."

You look up from the bottles and scan the immediate vicinity. "Amanda?"

"Sure enough. The face that launched a thousand trips to Bloomingdale's."

"Where?"

Tad puts his hand behind your head and directs your gaze to a group near the elevator. She is standing in profile, not twenty feet away. At first you think this is just a close resemblance, then she lifts her hand to her shoulder and begins to twirl a strand of hair between the tips of her fingers. Her agent used to tell her she'd ruin her hair that way. There is no doubt.

Not now, you think.

She's wearing toreador pants and a silver flak

jacket. Beside her, a Mediterranean hulk in a white silk shirt emanates a proprietary air. As you watch he smiles at something Amanda has said, and reaches over to squeeze her ass.

Au contraire, Pierre. Sexual Abandonment in spades.

The man looks like he was carved by Praxiteles in 350 B.C. and touched up by Paramount in 1947. You wonder if the physique is functional or cosmetic. How well would he respond if you ripped his ears off?

"Who's the greaseball?" Tad says.

You reach down for a bottle and pour yourself a large drink. "Must be lucky Pierre."

"I've seen him somewhere."

"Gentlemen's Quarterly."

"No. I've seen him around. I know it." Tad nods his head up and down, as if trying to dislodge a memory. "I saw him at a party. Note the coke spoon dangling betwixt his hairy pecs."

"I don't want to hear about it."

"He wasn't with Amanda. Some other bimbo."

Stevie returns from the bathroom. "Here's the dancing fool," she says.

"I don't need to dance to be foolish."

Tad says, "Batten down the hatches, Coach. She's coming at you."

Sure enough, here's Amanda.

She says, "*Ciao, bello,*" and before you can react she kisses your cheek.

Is she out of her mind? Doesn't she know that you desist from strangling her only through the exercise of heroic restraint?

She kisses Tad with the same formal benevolence. Tad introduces Stevie to Amanda. You can't even believe this is happening. Shouldn't someone say what a nice party this is?

"Is that your Italian stallion?" Tad says, nodding in the direction from which Amanda has come. "Or your Greek peak? Your French mensch? Or some other species of wetback?"

"That's Odysseus," Amanda says. "My fiancé."

"Odysseus," Tad says. "Odysseus. Right, the Greek." You wish Tad would shut up.

Amanda smiles at you as if you were an acquaintance whose name she is eager to remember. Won't she at least berate you for trying to trash her fashion show?

"So, how's it going?" she says. You stare at her, craving a glimmer of irony or shame in her big blue eyes.

"How's it going?" You start to laugh. She laughs too. You slap your thigh. She wants to know how it's going. A very funny question. Hilarious. Amanda is a riot. You are laughing so hard that you choke. Stevie slaps your back. As soon as you catch your breath you start laughing even harder. Amanda looks alarmed. She doesn't know how funny she can be. You want to tell her she's a barrel of monkeys but you can't speak. You are laughing. People are pounding your back. It's funny. People are funny. Everything's so funny you could die laughing. You can't breathe. You can't even see.

◪

"Drink," Tad says. He is holding you up with one arm and holding a plastic cup with the other. "Let there be space," Tad says to the faces around you. You don't see Amanda's.

"What's the matter," Stevie asks.

"He's epileptic," Tad says. "I know how to handle this." She retreats, understandably.

"I'm not epileptic," you say.

"No, just an emotional quadriplegic."

"I couldn't believe it," you say. *"How's it going?* Can you believe she said that?" You start to laugh again.

"Take a breather, Coach." Tad deposits you in a Mies van der Rohe chair. "You think *that's* funny," Tad says, "wait till you hear this."

"What?"

"Odysseus, right? You remember who he is?"

"How could I forget?"

"I finally figured out where I saw him before."

"With his hand on Amanda's ass."

"No. Listen to this. I have this account at the agency. No need to name names. But there's this old babe in Atlanta who runs a company and comes up to New York two or three times a year for a face lift and free meals on the agency's expense account. Naturally, she expects company for the evenings. So we provide this service through a little outfit called 'Dial a Hunk.' Male escort service, very top drawer. And when I say *escort* I am being uncharacteristically discreet. Anyway, about a year ago we dialed a hunk and *voilà* Odysseus."

"Don't try to cheer me up."

"It's true. I had to go out with these freaks two nights running, and needless to say the Allagash Express was derailed. The agency paid for his services, which definitely did not include witty conversation."

When you start to laugh, Tad says, "Careful." But it's under control.

"Dial a Hunk."

"That's it."

"Dial a Fucking Hunk."

"Now *that*," Tad says, "is funny. The wily Odysseus."

"Amanda's finally got the right number," you say, wishing you found it funnier. You wish this laughter could lift you out of your heavy body and carry you beyond this place, out through an open window and up over the city until all this ugliness and pain were reduced to a twinkling of faraway lights.

"I don't know," you say. "Actually, it's not that funny. It's just pathetic."

"Don't pour good sympathy after bad," Tad says.

"Where's Stevie?"

"That's another sob story. You want to steer clear of that, Coach."

"Why?"

"Stevie, aka Steve, had his third operation a few weeks ago. Convincing, isn't he?"

"You expect me to believe that?" You replay images of Stevie in your mind. "Bullshit."

"Would I lie? Ask Jimmy Q if you don't believe me. What do you think the scarf around the neck is for? You can't remove an Adam's apple."

You have no idea whether Tad is serious or not, having been taken in by him on numerous occasions. Your curiosity about Stevie's chromosomes is by now exhausted. It is too late in the night to care.

"I was going to tell you."

"Thanks." You stand up.

"Take it easy, Coach." He puts his arm around your shoulders.

"I just realized something."

"What's that?"

"You and Amanda would make a terrific couple."

"I suppose that means that you get Odysseus all to yourself."

"Later, Tad."

❏

A set of bedrooms is tucked away in a corner of the loft. The first two rooms are full of coke fiends and earnest conversers. The third is free, and a phone sits on a table beside the bed. You find the number in your wallet.

"What time is it?" Vicky says after you identify yourself. "Where are you?"

"It's late. I'm in New York. I just wanted to talk."

"Let me guess; you're with Tad."

"I *was* with Tad."

"It's a little late for a chat. Is something wrong?"

"I just wanted to tell you my mom died." You hadn't meant to be so abrupt. You are moving too fast.

"Oh, God," Vicky says. "I'm sorry. I didn't know she was . . . when?"

"A year ago." The Missing Person.

"A *year* ago?"

"I didn't tell you before so I wanted to tell you now. It seemed important."

"I'm sorry."

"It's all right. It's not so bad. I mean, it was." You can't manage to say what you mean. "I wish you could've met her. You would've hit it off. She had hair like yours. Not just that."

"I'm not sure what to say."

"There's something else I didn't tell you. I got married. Bad mistake, but it's all over. I wanted you to know, in case it makes a difference. I'm drunk. Do you think I should hang up?"

In the ensuing pause you can hear the faint hum of the long-distance wire. "Don't hang up," Vicky says. "I can't think of anything to say right now, but I'm here. I'm a little confused."

"I tried to block her out of my mind. But I think I owe it to her to remember."

"Wait. *Who?*"

"My mother. Forget my wife. I'm talking about my mother. I was thinking today, after she found out she had cancer, she was talking to Michael and me . . ."

"Michael?"

"That's my brother. She made us promise that if the pain became unbearable we'd help her, you know, end it all. We had this prescription for morphine so there was this option. But then it got really bad. I asked her and she said that when you were dying you had a responsibility to the living. I was amazed she said that, the way she felt. And I was just thinking that we have a responsibility to the dead—the living, I mean. Does this make any sense?"

"Maybe. I can't tell, really," Vicky says.

"Can I call tomorrow?"

"Yes, tomorrow. Are you sure you're all right?"

Your brain feels like it is trying to find a way out of your skull. And you are afraid of almost everything. "I'm fine."

"Get some sleep. Call me if you can't."

The first light of the morning outlines the towers of the World Trade Center at the tip of the island. You turn in the other direction and start uptown. There are cobbles on the street where the asphalt has worn through. You think of the wooden shoes of the first Dutch settlers on these same stones. Before that, Algonquin braves stalking game along silent trails.

You're not sure exactly where you are going. You don't feel you have the strength to walk home. You walk faster. If the sunlight catches you on the streets, you will undergo some terrible chemical change.

After a few minutes you notice the blood on your fingers. You hold your hand up to your face. There is blood on your shirt, too. You find a Kleenex in your jacket pocket and hold it to your nose. You advance with your head tilted back against your shoulders.

By the time you reach Canal Street, you think that you will never make it home. You look for taxis. A bum is sleeping under the awning of a shuttered shop. As you pass he raises his head and says, "God bless you and forgive your sins." You wait for the cadge but it doesn't come. You wish he hadn't said anything.

As you turn, what is left of your olfactory equipment sends a message to your brain: fresh bread. Somewhere they are baking bread. You can smell it, even through the nosebleed. You see bakery trucks loading in front of a building on the next block. You watch as bags of rolls are carried out onto the loading dock by a man with tattooed forearms. This man is already at work so that normal people can have fresh bread for their morning tables. The righteous people who sleep at night and eat eggs for breakfast. It is Sunday morning and you haven't eaten since . . . when? Friday night. As you approach, the smell of bread washes over you like a gentle rain. You inhale deeply, filling your lungs. Tears come to your eyes, and you feel such a rush of tenderness and pity that you stop beside a lamppost and hang on for support.

The smell of bread recalls you to another morning. You arrived home from college after driving half the night; you just felt like coming home. When you walked in, the kitchen was steeped in this same aroma. Your mother asked what the occasion was, and you said a whim. You asked if she was baking. "Learning to draw inferences at college, are we," you remember her asking. She said she had to find some way to keep herself busy now that her sons were taking off. You said that you hadn't left, not really. You sat down at the kitchen table to talk, and the bread soon started to burn. She had made bread only two other times that you could recall. Both times it had burned. You remember being proud of your mother then for never having submitted to the tyranny of the kitchen, for having other things on her mind. She cut you two thick slices of bread anyway. They were charred on the outside but warm and moist inside.

You approach the tattooed man on the loading dock. He stops working and watches you. There is something wrong with the way your legs are moving. You wonder if your nose is still bleeding.

"Bread." This is what you say to him, although you meant to say something more.

"What was your first clue?" he says. He is a man who has served his country, you think, a man with a family somewhere outside the city.

"Could I have some? A roll or something?"

"Get outa here."

"I'll trade you my sunglasses," you say. You take off your shades and hand them up to him. "Ray-Bans. I lost the case." He tries them on, shakes his head a few times and then takes them off. He folds the glasses and puts them in his shirt pocket.

"You're crazy," he says. Then he looks back into the warehouse. He picks up a bag of hard rolls and throws it at your feet.

You get down on your knees and tear open the bag. The smell of warm dough envelops you. The first bite sticks in your throat and you almost gag. You will have to go slowly. You will have to learn everything all over again.

ABOUT THE AUTHOR

Jay McInerney is the author of two novels, *Bright Lights, Big City* and *Ransom*. His work has appeared in such publications as *Esquire*, *The New York Times*, *The Paris Review*, *Granta*, *Vanity Fair*, *Ms.*, *Vogue*, and *The New Republic*. *Bright Lights, Big City* has been translated into fourteen languages.